THE QUEST

KARINA KANTAS

ASTERI
PRESS

THE QUEST

© Karina Kantas 2018

Cover Art by Sharon Lipman from Fantasia Covers
https://www.facebook.com/FantasiaCovers

First published in 2019 by Bolide Publishing

http://bolidepublishing.com/asteri

ISBN: 978-1-912996-04-9

TITLES BY KARINA KANTAS:

Illusional Reality
Illusional Reality

The Outlaw Series
In Times of Violence
Huntress
Lawless Justice
Road Rage

Collections
Heads & Tales
Undressed

CONTENTS

THE QUEST

BOOK 2 OF ILLUSIONAL REALITY

AND SO IT BEGINS

Haty pulled a handful of weeds out of a crack between two old paving stones and stood to rub her back. She groaned as she looked at the rest of the patio. There was still so much to do. She knelt back down and dug the metal gardening fork into a cluster of Dandelions. A rustle from the bushes lining the west wall caught her attention. She glanced up, squinting in the heat of the sun. There was no wind; no reason for the sound. She waited for a cat or squirrel to run out, but the crunch of leaves and twigs told her something much heavier had crushed the debris.

"Danny!"

She threw the fork aside and jumped to her feet, clutching the garden chair for support. Her knuckles turned white as she surveyed the wall of foliage. They were moving. Something or someone was trying to push its way through. Her heart pounded, forcing a rush of blood to her head.

Her security detail rushed through the patio door

with his gun drawn. "Get inside."

Haty charged through the living room, and almost collided with the hallway door. She slammed it shut as she ran into the kitchen and yanked the cutlery drawer open, before spying the wooden block with the kitchen knives. She grabbed the chef's chopping knife. It would be no competition against Danny's Glock, but she was in survival mode. She crept back to the living room and hid behind the couch, straining to hear what was going on outside.

"Come out slowly," Danny barked. "Who are you? What are you doing here?"

There was a mumbled response, followed by Danny threatening physical violence, and then silence. Haty gripped the knife in both hands to keep it steady, thinking the worst when footsteps approached. It had to be a Senx. They had come for her before and she had nearly died. She wouldn't allow them to hurt her again, and especially not now, when she had so much more to lose.

She held her breath as the footsteps closed in but released it when Danny glanced wide-eyed at her and stepped back. "Woah." She jumped as he held his hands in the air and gulped. "Hey, it's me. It's okay. He's gone now."

"I … I …"

Danny eased the knife out of her hands and knelt beside her. "It's okay, you're safe." He pulled her into a hug. Yet Haty was frozen, unable to lean into his warm body. Unable to feel safe.

"Jeez, Haty, you're shaking."

Pushing him away, she looked up into his face.

"W-who was it?"

"Just a tramp looking for food."

"He must have been d-desperate to push his way through the brambles. I-I mean wasn't that the reason Sam planted them. To s-stop anyone from getting through?" Haty's body shivered as her mind played out what could happen if it a Senx had found its way to her.

"Yeah, I'll get the boss to look into that. Why don't you go upstairs? I'll make you a cuppa."

Haty nodded and made her way to the staircase. She gripped the wooden banister and walked slowly up the stairs, her legs still shaking. At the top of the landing she took a left and entered the bedroom at the rear of the upper floor. She had made her home her sanctuary and until now she'd been secure and felt safe and just that one unfortunate incident, had ripped that safety net to shreds. Dread filled her stomach, leaving her feeling sick.

She lay on her bed and curled up on her side, holding her stomach. She couldn't stop shaking. Her mind wandered but a tap on the bedroom door brought her back to reality.

Danny grinned. "How are you doing?" He handed Haty the mug of tea and she took a sip, winced, and placed the scolding tea on the bedside table.

"I overreacted." She faked a smile. "I'm sorry."

"No, I don't think you did. I just wish I knew who you are afraid of. I could help."

"It's complicated, Danny, and I'm not ready to talk about it yet. Please, you have to respect my decision." If she had to, she would remind him who was boss. Thya was stubborn and knew how to make herself heard. As a ruler it was one of the roles she played. Thya, gosh, she hadn't thought of her real name for such a long time. Using it now took her to a place and time she'd hoped to forget.

"Haty, are you okay? Haty?"

She blinked. "Sorry, what did you say?"

"I lost you for a moment there. Are you sure you're, all right?'

"I'm good. I'm just tired," she lied.

"Yeah, you work too hard. Eighteen hours most days. You should make more time for yourself."

She tilted her head. "You're counting? I guess I hoped to bury myself in my work, so I wouldn't have to think about things."

"Your past?"

She shrugged. "I'm trying to build a safe and happy life for me and Alex."

"Except you've never felt safe, even with the 24/7 security Sam provides you with. It's like you're expecting someone to attack."

"And you watch too much!"

Danny stiffened. "Just doing my job, ma'am."

That stung. "Danny, I'm sorry. I didn't mean to snap."

"No, it's all right. You've been through a lot. It's okay. Look, I'm going to go now. Just know that I'm here and I won't let anyone hurt you. You have my promise." Danny seemed to be waiting for a response from her but, when none came, he sighed and left the room, pulling the door shut behind him.

Haty reached over for the tea. Her hands still shook, so she gripped hold of the mug before taking a sip. It was a little cooler now, though tasteless. Time froze as the room shifted from her bedroom to a scene she'd hoped to never live through again. She stood in front of the carved, marble throne, looking down at the Tsinian council. Alkazar, her tutor, her love, stood before her in chains. His head bent, refusing to look her in the eye.

"No!" she yelled and threw the cup. It smashed against the bedroom wall, pulling her back to the present. She was left panting and her tears flowing.

Danny rushed into the room without knocking. "What happened?' He bent down to pick up the pieces of the broken cup.

"Leave it! Danny, just go, please. I need to be alone."

He frowned, pursing his lips, and then left without saying another word.

Haty sat up and grabbed Alex's teddy from the edge of the bed. She leaned over and hugged it. Her breath trembled as she fought to keep the memories at bay.

The Senx could come for her and Alex at any time and there would be nothing Danny, or his boss, Sam, could do to stop them. The life she had built would be taken away – again.

Tears rolled down her cheek and she brushed them away. *Get a grip woman. You're stronger than this. Remember who you are – remember your heritage.*

***

Haty was putting her clean socks away in the dresser when she noticed a subtle glow from the back of the drawer. Sweat formed on her neck as she reached inside and pulled a black cord necklace out. It wasn't the jewellery making her anxious, it was the reason the necklace was glowing. No matter how hard she wished she was seeing things, there was no mistaking the warning.

She held up the offending necklace with two fingers and stared at the crystal. Omad came to mind. As did the rest of the Tsinian council and others she had grown close to. The heart-breaking farewell played out as she recalled walking down the line and saying goodbye, taking the gifts of jewels they offered. Athron offered her hope, although there was none left. Pertius, who she had spent hours with, reading scrolls as they searched for a clause to the most serious regulation of the Tsinian code. And finally, Omad, who looked like an ageing wizard without the pointy hat. He had given Haty the opal-coloured crystal prism and informed her that it would glow when a Tsinian stepped foot on Earth. There was one person missing, the most important Tsinian to her. But he was no more. His life was taken as punishment for murdering his wife and unborn child. Still, Haty never believed he was capable of such a heinous crime. And yet he confessed. Haty shook her head at the memory and wiped her wet cheek.

Had she stopped wearing the necklace in the hope that she would eventually forget who she was? This was impossible, of course. Alex was a constant reminder of Tsinia and of her love, Alkazar, especially when he looked at her, the smile, the twinkle in his eye, questionably, exactly like his father had. Alex was her last link to Alkazar, and she loved the boy more than anything else. Without him, she would have given up long ago.

How long had the crystal been glowing? Hours? Days?

She closed her eyes, yet the brightness penetrated her eyelids. No, there was no mistake. Resigned to the fact that she could not ignore the warning, she opened her eyes and sat on the edge of the bed, glaring at the crystal before dropping it as though it burnt her fingers.

A Tsinian was on Earth searching for her. Did she have enough time to send Alex away? What if the crystal worked like a homing device? She could destroy it or hide it somewhere. That might give her enough time, but no, she couldn't do that. The crystal was probably worth more than she could make in a lifetime, and Omad had given it to her as a gift. She couldn't destroy it. Besides, she had given her oath that if they needed her, she would return.

"Well, Omad, my friend, I will see you soon." Wiping away the tears, she let out a long breath.

She couldn't waste any more time daydreaming. The last time a Tsinian came looking for her, Senx had followed, and it was highly likely they would do so now. If she was dead, there would be no stopping them from ruling Tsinia and taking the power of the Changlins – the sacred stones that represented each of the elements.

And then there was the reason for their visit. It wasn't to say "Hi". Either her kinsman needed her or - worse - the Tsinian council had learned about Alex. She would have to return to a land she'd hoped to never see again, and to a past she'd wanted to forget.

"Alex, Alex, Alex," she whispered. She picked up her phone and speed-dialled Sam Craine's office number. She had grown close to the owners of the security team over the last few years. It wasn't so much a working relationship, more like they were looking out for an older sister. She would often be invited to their houses for dinner, or a girl's shopping trip with the women. Christmas dinners were always the same. Dinner at Sam's house with his wife and his two boys Ryan and Philip. Danny joined them too, along with his working partner Trevor and his fiancée Janice.

"Sam, it's Haty. I'm getting Trevor to pick Alex up from the nursery and bring him to your office. You have to take him to my parents' house. I need to leave. I'm not sure how long I will be gone, but Alex can never come back to this house. Do you understand? You know what must be done …"

"Has something happened? Are you in any danger?"

"No." Haty paused, as she felt the hairs on her arms stand up.

"Haty, where's Trevor? Haty?"

Haty shook out of her daze. "Please, just do what I ask. Make sure the house is locked up tight and send that email to all my clients. My lawyer will handle the rest." She paused. "Look after him, Sam. Make sure he's well and happy."

"How long do you plan to be away?'

"Not too long, I hope."

"Don't you think it's about time you told me what's going on?"

"I can't. It's… complicated."

"Damn it, woman! You know me well enough to trust me by now."

His volume rose and rightly so, after all the time

they had spent together, Christmas with the family, days out with the kids, she should trust him. She did, but he would never believe her. Who would?

"Of course, I trust you. It's just… Look, I can't talk about this right now; I haven't the time."

Sam sighed deeply. "The next time we meet you're going to tell me everything."

"When I get back, I promise. Watch over my son. Goodbye."

Haty closed the phone before he could demand more answers from her. She owed Sam and his team an explanation, but it had never been the right time, especially now. She went into the bathroom to splash cold water on her face and neck. But when she looked in the mirror, she didn't like what stared back. "Snap out of it," she cursed. "Remember who you are!"

She took a deep breath, adjusted her top and patted her hair down, then rushed into Alex's room and shoved his clothes into a rucksack.

Haty shouted down to Trevor and he bounded up the stairs. His large frame blocked the doorway. "What's up?"

"I need you to pick Alex up from the nursery and take him to the office. Sam's waiting for you. And call Danny. I need him here."

His brow tightened. "Is everything okay?"

"Not really. Promise me you will guard Alex well. Now is the time for extra vigilance. Tell him – tell him mummy loves him and kiss him for me. I don't think I will have time to say goodbye."

She couldn't imagine not seeing him again, holding her sweet boy in her arms. No matter how strong she pretended to be, she couldn't control her emotions. Her shoulders dropped, her knees bent, and she slumped to the floor. Turning her head aside, she cried.

Trevor stepped forward. "Hey now, tell me what I can do to help. I hate to see you like this."

"I'm sorry." She sniffed. "I can't. Please, Trevor, go now. Take him straight to the office. If I have time I will come and say goodbye. Tell Alex I love him, and that Mummy will be home soon. And, Trevor, be careful."

"Do you need extra protection?"

She shook her head. "Alex needs the protection now. Take this rucksack. Sam will pick up the rest of his things later. Go – now."

She held out the bag but couldn't bring herself to look him in the eye.

Trevor took the rucksack in one hand and, with the other, pulled her off the floor and held her in a tight embrace.

"It cuts me up to see you like this, girl," he said. "It hurts that you don't trust me enough to tell me what's going on. I know we agreed on a need to know basis, but God damn it, Haty, I need to know! You're like family."

She pushed herself out of the embrace. "Please, go. I can't waste any more time."

"Just promise me you'll take care of yourself and stay in contact."

Haty smiled but didn't answer. If he knew where she was going, he would know she wouldn't be able to keep in touch. She watched him bound down the stairs and then sat in the middle of the bedroom floor, staring at Alex's toys littering the side of his room.

Danny found her staring into space and clutching onto the teddy.

He knelt beside her. "I guess it's time. So, what do we do now?"

Haty rose to her feet. "I need some fresh air. I'm going for a walk"

"I have the car outside. I'll take you anywhere you want to go."

"No, Danny. Someone is looking for me. If it's who I think it is, they need to find me." She shuddered and hoped he wouldn't ask any more questions.

"Has this got anything to do with the government? The secret service?"

Haty shook her head. "I suppose with all the secrecy you would think that." Any other time she would have laughed at the absurdity of the situation. "No, it's nothing to do with the government. Please, Danny, can we just drop it?"

"Yeah, sure." He shrugged his shoulders.

"I'm going to grab my jacket then we'll leave, okay?" She didn't wait for his answer before running down the stairs.

Once everything was locked up, she handed him the keys. "We'll walk towards town. I want to see Alex if I have time."

He nodded. "Where are you going?"

"I can't tell you."

"But you've got no money. No clothes. Nothing."

"Where I'm going, I do not need those things."

Danny stopped walking and swung her around to face him. "Haty, our relationship has been built around secrecy and I'm getting pretty pissed off with it, especially now! Forget that I'm a paid bodyguard. I'm your friend too. I want to help."

She pulled away from him. "I know you do, and I'm sorry. When I return — *if* I return – I promise I will tell you everything. Although you won't believe me when I do."

"Let me be the judge of that." He glanced at her, as though trying to read her thoughts, but she wasn't giving anything away. So, he shrugged his shoulders and continued walking.

Haty hoped Sam wouldn't take Alex straight to her parents, and they would be at the office when she arrived. If she had time, she needed to see him before she left. Just to smell his hair and touch his cheek.

Her parents weren't Alex's blood relatives. Haty had been adopted when she was only a few months old. She had been found abandoned outside the doors of the children's home, barely a few days old. Her adoptive parents had been on the register for quite some time and adopted her immediately, christening her as Becky. She had learned about her adoption when she was sixteen, but it wasn't until her fateful arrival in Tsinia, that she learnt who her real parents were. Ganties, the rulers of Tsinia, a magical world beyond this one. An oracle had prophesized that Darthorn, warlord of Senx, would attack their city. When the fighting commenced, her parents took her to the nearest orb, located just outside their borders. They went unguarded and were killed, but not before they sent Haty to Earth.

She didn't get any further than the bottom of the road before her skin prickled and the hairs on her arms stood up. She turned around sharply, certain that someone was following. Danny straightened his back and looked around.

The street was empty. Haty pulled out the crystal and was amazed to see it not only shone brighter but pulsated.

Danny stared at the crystal, mesmerized by it. "How - how's it doing that?"

"It works like a beacon." She placed the crystal in his hand. "We will wait here."

Danny nodded, his hand poised on his holstered gun as they waited for God knew what.

An old man in an outdated, grey three-piece suit appeared from around the corner. *Salco.* He had come for her the first time and saved her life. Haty smiled. His eyes lit up with delight and he bounded towards her. Danny drew his gun.

Haty grabbed Danny's hand. "It's okay. I know this man."

Though he holstered the weapon, his hand remained on the butt. He wasn't the type that liked the unexpected, and Haty imagined the situation was strange to him.

Salco stopped in front of her and glanced at Danny. He held his hands out in front of him. "I come in peace." He held Haty at arm's length, smiling as he looked her up and down. "My lady, tis an honour to sight you again."

"Can you give me a moment here, Danny?"

She pulled Salco to the side. Danny screwed his face into a frown as he stepped away, although his gaze never left them.

"Well met, Salco, my good friend, how pleasant it

is to lay sight upon you. I hoped it would be you that appeared. You have not aged at all!"

He stared, puzzled by her last remark. Haty smiled. She had forgotten Tsinian speech was different from what she was used to. They did not live their lives with time, days, or ages. "You appear identical to when I previously sighted you."

Salco smiled. "And you, my princess, appear more radiant than ever, although I do not hold fondness to your mane."

Haty nodded and thought about her appearance on Tsinia. Her skin there was soft, young, and glowing. Her hair was long and silky to the touch, but the strangest change was the colour. Upon Tsinian soil, it changed to a shade of silver, notorious with Ganties. On Earth, she was a brunette and kept it tied up in a ponytail.

"What of Tsinia?" she asked. "I assume you are not here for pleasure?"

"Nay, my lady, I am not. I long that my appearance was under different circumstances. Omad has forbidden me to discuss with you the happenings on Tsinia. Nevertheless, I have been dispatched to transport you back to your home, if your oath still stands? Your kinsmen desperately require aid. We attempted to control the difficulty yet have failed. Will you make yourself available to us?"

"With certainty. I am prepared for departure."

Salco smiled and bowed his head. "Very good, my lady, the orb is in close proximity."

Haty, nodded. She walked over to Danny, who was looking understandably bewildered.

"What's Tsinia and why did he call you my lady? Haty, what the hell is going on?"

"I'm leaving with Salco. Don't worry, he's a good friend and I'll be well protected."

Danny looked Salco up and down, his eyebrows rising, and his lips pursed. "Is this who you were expecting?"

"Yes, it is, and now I must go." She held Danny's arm and steered him further away from Salco. "Look after Alex for me. Promise me that and tell him I love him."

Danny nodded. "I promise."

She walked away, willing herself not to cry.

"I wish you would tell me where you're going, damn it!" Danny shouted after her.

"Worry not, sir, our lady will be cared for well," Salco said.

Salco and Haty turned the corner. She didn't waste any time questioning Salco. "It would be prudent to inform me to what has occurred for the requirement of my aid. I would prefer to be prepared rather than surprised."

"My lady, naught could prepare you."

"How so?" Haty stopped walking. "I demand you reveal everything to me."

Salco sighed heavily. "If you insist, only I will not be held responsible for the outcome."

Haty nodded. "So be it."

"Kovon has returned."

She shook her head. "Tis not possible. How can this be?"

"There is further. He has an increase in strength

and retains the power of the dark force. My lady, we ought not to delay."

Haty shook herself out of her stupor and continued walking, although it felt as though it was a dream. The last time she had seen Kovon, he was blind, deaf, and without speech. How could he have recovered from such inflictions?

"Is it safe to return? Is the orb protected?" Salco didn't reply. "Do not hold back from me. Is Tsinia protected from the Senx?"

Salco looked to the floor. "I hoped I would not be the one to inform you…"

Sweat lined her palms and she swallowed hard as she waited for him to reply.

"Kovon has seized Tsinia. He currently rules Senx and our land."

Haty stepped back as though someone had taken a clenched fist and soccer punched her. She swallowed bile before replying. "Nay, this cannot have happened. Was not the city defended? Why was I not informed as soon as the threat was noticed?"

"Omad detained much duration, for he knew of your dislike to return. My lady, are you unwell? Your skin is ashen. We must hurry to Valcan."

"'Tis true I never wanted to return, even so, I bestowed an oath that I would, should you be in requirement of your princess. You ought not to have delayed."

She didn't want to ask but needed to know. "Does Kovon retain the power of the sacred stones? Where are the Changlins located? What of my kinsmen, how do they fare?"

"We are concealed within the Caves of Celdor upon the Outlands, the Changlins remain with us. We dare not venture into our city."

Haty took a quivering breath. "Were there many losses?"

"We were forewarned of Kovon's attack by an oracle. We were as prepared as was possible. Even so, Kovon attacked Tsinia with an army belonging to a race we had yet to sight. They possessed strength far greater than our own and we could not contend. There were too many. Even with the employment of our gifts, we were outnumbered and so fled. Twenty-one fell, including three of the council."

Haty stopped walking and stared at Salco as she imagined what life must be like for her gentle kinsmen. Then she started again at a quicker pace. Words would not come but one thing she knew: that she needed to get back to Tsinia as soon as possible. She was the protector of the land and should never have left. They were her kinsmen. Tsinia was her homeland. Oh, how the gentle folk had suffered.

The rest of the journey was spent in silence. They arrived at a road of garages. They were all shut, apart from one whose door was ajar. Salco slid the door to the side and Haty followed him inside. A shimmering bubble of swirls and wisps awaited them. She had no second thoughts about stepping into the bright light of the orb. Her kinsmen needed her. She felt no fear, no apprehension, just a sense of eagerness and a familiar feeling of revenge.

THE GATHERING

Thya and Salco arrived in a field of golden grass. Where was Tsinia, and why couldn't she see the momentous trees the Tsinians lived in? How far were they from the city? And where were Omad and the council?

Her skin tingled as her nails grew and the skin on her hands became softer and line free. The band around her ponytail snapped and her hair grew in length, changing from a deep brunette to light silver. Salco smiled as she took a breath of Enumac air. Every gulp awoke her senses, making her stronger and more determined. Her dormant power was awakening, pulsating and coursing through her body. As her power increased so did the heat within. Closing her eyes, she opened her arms wide and laughed as the sensation washed over her. Holding her head up, and with her arms and hands stretched out in front of her, she willed a large boulder around five meters away to move. It took a few seconds to feel in control. When she opened her eyes, she didn't just see the rock moving, it was suspended in the air as though it weighed nothing. Salco clapped enthusiastically and she lost her concentration. The rock crashed to the ground, causing a flume of dusty smoke to fill the air. She turned her face aside before dust got into her eyes.

"Wonderful," he cried, and then turned and started walking north.

Thya smiled and kicked off her shoes as she felt the soles tighten and the skin harden.

Now it didn't matter the terrain. However, the texture of the golden grass she stood on was soft and bouncy and reminded her of an English garden. "Alex..." she whispered.

"Rightly so," Salco called, and fumbled with the laces of his Hushpuppies, puffing with exasperation as he then tried taking them off from the heel. Thya laughed as this white-haired, short bearded man, dressed like he was going to a wedding, hopping around in a circle, shaking his leg like a dog. She walked towards him, ready to offer her help, but he had taken them off and thrown them as far away as he could by the time she got to him. Thya shook her head and giggled.

They walked for at least an hour through a field of tiny yellow flowers. Thya breathed in the fresh floral scent and, together with the brilliant white of the Enumac sky, a vision of England in summer appeared and she watched herself in her garden playing with Alex.

As they continued their journey, the terrain changed suddenly, as did the atmosphere. It matched her solemn mood. Thya shivered as the sky turned grey and a chill crept through her. A misty fog surrounded them, and sharp stones and rocks lay before her. Thya wanted to ask him why the orb hadn't taken them closer to the caves. It would have cut out this long and often difficult trek, but she concluded that, as they were hidden, they would be worrying about Kovon finding out about them using an orb and possibly compromising their safety. She thought about them fleeing their land and how they would have coped, journeying to the caves unaided. The cold and grey was the opposite of the warmth and sunshine of Tsinia they were used to.

As they entered through a stone gateway built into a wall of rock, Salco pointed out the Caves of Celdor. A huge grey mountain lined the horizon, resulting in a lengthy and difficult climb. At first, Thya regretted throwing her shoes away. The sharp stones hurt her feet, no matter how hard her soles were. But then she remembered her kinsmen had made the same journey, so she suffered in silence.

She recognized Omad as soon as she saw him. He wore the same long grey robe from before, and still sported a lengthy grey beard, only this time, he'd let someone braid it. He stood outside the mouth of the cave, waiting for their arrival.

"Thya, my lady, you are well?"

"Extremely. Tis good to lay sight upon you, my fine friend." She embraced him and then stroked his beard braid. She took a step back and raised her eyebrows. "Why was I not informed of these occurrences? Why did you not send for me before this?"

Omad's sight fell on Salco. "Has Salco informed you of the tragic occurrence, even though I bade him not to? Tis my error alone, my lady." He bowed his head and held his arm out.

Thya smiled and took Omad's arm. He led her into the Celdor Cavern, taking her down a narrow tunnel lit with bright flames from torches. The cave was surprisingly warm and dry, nothing like the cold, damp and smelly caves in England. Again, the thought of her past life rushed back at her and she shook her head to clear it from her mind and return to the present. She needed to concentrate on where she was now and whatever task faced her.

Omad led her to a large dark wooden door which split into two openings. Salco stepped forward and opened it.

Thya was stunned at the sight. She turned her head as she took everything in. Small wooden tables were dotted around a huge, surprisingly brightly lit cavern. There was no fire blazing and yet the cavern was warm and welcoming, with light coming from chandeliers of candles. Thya smiled as she watched groups of Tsinians sitting together. Some were eating, reading, or practicing magic, while others casually chatted or laughed. Thya wanted to laugh with them. She wanted to sit and involve herself with their conversations but, before she had time to step further inside, someone saw her and gasped. The chatter stopped and silence followed. She wondered if they were waiting for her to speak. Glancing around the room, she searched for familiar faces. Someone clapped and then another, and quickly the applause turned to cheers which grew in volume, echoing off the walls. She took in their happiness and love and smiled. It turned into laughter as they came towards her in a sea of smiling faces, eyes lit with happiness. They hugged one another and seemed to need to touch her or at least her clothing. She supposed her tight jeans must have looked odd to them. Thya reached out and grabbed every hand she could, making sure they knew she was real and not an illusion.

She understood why they crowded her but, even so, she craved space to breathe. She had no idea her presence would cause so much emotion for them or herself. Salco took her arm and led her away from the overly zealous crowd.

Thya stayed for a short while and was given berry juice and pastries. Although she ate, she had no appetite. The Tsinians celebrated with song and merry cheer. She knew what they were thinking - that she would again save them, and all would be well and peaceful. The truth was, she didn't have a clue as to how to proceed, what she needed to do, or if she still had the power to defeat Kovon. She should have never allowed him to live. Thoughts of hitting and hurting something or someone came into her mind. She looked at her fists. They were clenched so tightly the skin had turned white.

She squeezed her eyes tightly shut, concentrating on slowing her racing heart and regulating her breathing.

"Lady Thya, are you well?"

She opened her eyes. Omad peered at her, his head tilted as he waited for her answer.

"We sit idly by while Kovon resides in the Escos – my home – bathing in the pure waters of Tsinia?"

Omad dropped his head.

She hadn't meant to speak those words aloud. It was intended as a private thought.

"Pardon," she said, "I am anxious to converse with

the council. Have them convene immediately."

"It shall be done," Omad answered with a bow.

Thya was led out of the cavern and down another narrow tunnel into a smaller cave. Huge **stalactites** hung impressively from the cavern's ceiling. With what she'd seen so far, the work the Tsinians had done to the caves must have taken a very long time. She had been gone nearly four years. So how long had they been in Celdor Caverns? How long ago did they flee from their land?

Some of the council were seated on chiselled out rock made into tall arched-back chairs. The rest of the Tsinian Council followed her into the cavern. They bowed respectfully and took their seats.

"My lady," Omad said, and signalled for her to sit in the last seat.

They sat in silence until Athorn entered.

"My lady," he greeted. "It was believed that your gifts alone could defeat Kovon, although recently I received an oracle."

"Decipher," she called.

"There is not another means to conquer Kovon, other than with the employment of the Darkeye."

Thya shook her head. "I destroyed the eye in Senx. Kovon warned me not to destroy it. He understood that I would be in requirement of its power, only I ignored him. I was certain he spoke in jest. My stubbornness has destroyed our only chance to conclude the conflict." She sighed and bowed her head.

"That would be so if another Darkeye did not exist."

She rose from her seat. "Another? Inform me."

"There is a duplicate. Tis housed in the city of Helkon."

Thya turned to Omad. "Where is this city? I will depart at once."

"Helkon is within the Outlands," Omad said. "The difficulty is that we are without awareness of the land. This would not prevent us from attempting to locate the Darkeye, if not for the Oracle stating that only the heir of Tsinia could locate and employ the Darkeye."

"I am your saviour and tis down to me alone to deliver you all."

"Tis not accurate, my lady," Athron said.

"Clarify?".

"If you do not retrieve the Darkeye's twin and defeat Kovon, then tis prophesied that all of Enumac would be ruled by Kovon and his armies. So tis written, so it will be done."

Thya took a deep breath. "He needs to be destroyed once and for all. There will be no mercy this time. And you state there is none that retain knowledge of the Outlands?"

"There is not, to my awareness, my lady," Omad answered, "though I am resolved to arrange an escort of Tsinians with suitable attributes. They will accompany and aid you on your quest."

"Nay, Omad, though I am grateful. The only place I will receive assistance is in conference with the Changlins."

"Tis fitting," he said. "I will direct you to where they dwell."

The Changlins, five oval stones each representing an element, were the source of the Tsinians' power. On her first visit to Tsinia, she learnt she had a unique gift, and was the only Tsinian who could connect with the Changlins. They spoke through her, advised her, and aided in the defeat of Kovon. She hoped they would help again.

Omad led her to their resting place deeper within the caves. She waited for him to leave her then knelt silently before them and waited for the stones to acknowledge her. A powerful force hit her chest, almost knocking her backwards. She felt a deep pressure pushing within her and yet it wasn't painful or uncomfortable, it was just new. The pressure lightened, and a warmth rose within her. Thya experienced the feeling of ecstasy. Taking a deep breath, she allowed the power of the Changlins to take over.

If you're to regain control of Tsinia and defeat Kovon, you must go to Helkon, the inner voice said.

For the first time since hearing the deep booming voice that seemed to vibrate off her bones, Thya realized that the Changlins spoke in her own native tongue. But why should they speak in English and not Tsinian? She brushed the thought aside as the Changlins continued.

You are to travel with three Tsinians. They must volunteer as your companions. You are not to approach them.

"I understand."

Travel through the Forest of Illusions until you reach a crossroad. Your heart will tell you which path to take. Do not think this quest will be easy. There will be danger and death. However, should you reach Helkon, you will be given the truth to all the questions that plague you. Stay strong, Thya. Listen to your heart and never give up hope.

Thya stood up and brushed the dirt from her clothes. "And the Darkeye? Where in the city is it?"

The inner voice remained silent. The connection had been cut, leaving her to lean against the stone wall until the weakness subsided.

THE CHOSEN

The council was standing in groups talking quietly when she returned. "I wish to address my kinsmen. All of them." She turned and left without waiting for their reply and made her way back to the cavern where she knew her subjects would be anxiously waiting.

Quiet murmurs ceased when she entered and walked to a raised ledge on the far right of the cavern. Pertius, the tutor of the code, held open a familiar bag. She reached inside and took a pinch of the gold sprinkles. She patted it on her lips, before smiling and nodding to Pertius. Salco stood by the ledge and held his hand out. He helped her onto the ledge and she looked out at the sea of worried faces, which only added to her resolve to end Kovon and take back their beautiful land.

"You all retain awareness on why I return and of the quest prophesied by the ancient oracles." Her voice rang loud and clear.

Many of the Tsinians nodded their heads in answer.

"There are three chosen to accompany me on the quest for the Darkeye. You are required to present yourself, freely, to me. Only Tsinians that are resolved to proceed can bestow their services, and only those that were named will be permitted to come. In the coming of light, the chosen will commence our journey. Be aware and think prudently prior to stepping forward. The quest will be perilous. I bestow an oath to use my power and give my last breath if need be, to destroy Kovon and his army and take back Tsinia, our land, our home. You are my witnesses."

"Praise to the Changlins," voices sang out. "Praise to Thya our queen and saviour," called others.

Thya held up her hand and there was silence. "Nay, save the praise for when it is earned. I pray to the Changlins that your duration will not be long. Now, I smell the aroma of baked pastries, so let us feast together and praise the Changlins for the shelter and good cheer we possess."

Omad held out his hand, waiting to help her down from the ledge. She smiled and stepped down.

"My lady, I am, as always, available to you. I trust I could be of service through your difficult journey and I pray to the Changlins that the name Omad was one of the chosen." His head tilted slightly as he waited for her response.

Thya smiled and took his hands into hers. "My dear friend, I would not want this any other way. The name Omad was indeed spoken. And how wonderful it was to perceive it."

Omad let out a deep breath. She tried not to laugh,

and it came out as a chuckle.

Thya took his arm and they walked through the cavern. She nodded and smiled at the Tsinians' greetings and praise for her return.

"Somewhere along the route, Omad, you retain a purpose. I am not aware of when or how, only that without you, we cannot fulfil this quest. Zarc is awarded the title of the head of the council in your absence and will govern my kinsmen until your return."

Omad raised his eyebrows.

"Until *we* return," she corrected, and smiled, although it was false. She hadn't given it much thought but, once they secured the Darkeye and its power, once Tsinia was nurtured and returned to how it once was, she would return home to Alex.

"If tis your command," Omad said, looking puzzled.

The way he stared, she wondered how much of her he could read.

"'Tis," she replied, and this time her beaming smile was genuine.

"Very well, my lady, it will be done."

Food and drink appeared on the tables, which had been placed in two long lines on either side of the cavern. With every Tsinian doing their part, the arrangement took a matter of moments. The cavern was soon full of song and merry cheer again. As the feast continued, many Tsinians came to where were she sat and offered their service to her. All were turned away but thanked graciously. She hid her giggle behind cupped hands when some of the volunteers didn't hide how relieved they were. One had mopped his sweating brow while thanking her repeatedly. Another let out a deep sigh and some tried to hide their smiles at the good news.

Athron was one of the few Tsinians that seemed put out that he wasn't needed on the quest.

Thya stood up and stepped close to him, looking him in the eye. "Good Athron, should your name have been bestowed, I would have refused." Athron gasped but she continued, nonetheless. "I would have refused as my kinsmen are in requirement of their reader of oracles. Should there be another attack, should Kovon discover where you are, how are they to be fair-warned and escape? Nay, my kinsmen require you more than I, at least on this quest. You can be sure there will be further. Now go, enjoy the feast. Your courage will not be forgotten."

She spotted Valcan making his way towards her at a slow gait. She had no doubt that his wondrous gift of healing would be useful, but he was too frail for such a journey, having aged greatly since their last meeting.

"My lady," Valcan panted, and then pulled himself up on his staff. "I surrender all to the cause and if by chance I am required and called forth, then I proceed willingly."

"I am certain you would, Valcan. However, you are not named and if you were, I would refuse. You are not as agile as you once were. Tis prudent for you to remain and aid your kinsmen. Suppose they require a healer?"

Valcan shook his head. "Would it not be beneficial to include a healer among you?"

Thya opened her mouth to speak when another voice rang out.

"Permit me to assist you on your journey."

A young Tsinian stepped out from behind Valcan.

"My lady," Valcan said, "tis my honour to introduce you to my son."

The young Tsinian bowed to Thya, knelt, and kissed her hand gently.

"My lady, tis a great thrill to lay sight upon you, for my father remarks of you constantly. It would be an honour if you would accept me as one of your companions. I am a gifted healer and I am certain, as are you, that you will require a healer on your journey."

Thya laughed. "A son. My, you have been busy. No wonder you have aged."

"My lady?"

Remembering herself and Tsinian speech, she waved her hand and looked down at the Tsinian kneeling in front of her.

"The decision is not mine. Declare to me, what are you named?"

"I am Somal, my lady."

She studied him carefully. He looked strong and capable, but she wondered how much knowledge and understanding lay behind those brown eyes. She guessed him to be in his late twenties. Could one so young have the skillset and gift needed for the journey?

"Arise, Somal. We have not encountered, and yet your name is familiar to me for you are one of the chosen. If you are certain tis your desire to travel an unexplored road and face the unknown, then I accept your labour."

"I am resolved, my lady." He bowed and left her table to join a group of Tsinians similar in age. They patted his back. One ruffled his hair, and another shook his hand. Valcan smiled and stood up straight, with his chest puffed out like a proud peacock. It seemed being chosen for a perilous journey was quite an honour.

Thya looked around at the faces. There were some she did not recognize, others she knew but not well, and familiar ones that had aged. She still found it strange that she wouldn't see a single child among her kinsmen. It was hard to believe that Tsinians, once born, would be a child but for a Tril moon – the equivalent to a single Earth day. On the second day, the child would become of age – sixteen Earth years – and able to master the code and begin their tutoring of the arts. She thought it sad for the parents and the Tsinian to miss out on the fun of childhood. Her thoughts returned to Alex and the sweet memories they had made. Tears escaped, and she quickly brushed them away, but not before Somal noticed and walked over to her, gently touching her shoulder.

"My Lady, you need respite. It has been a challenging time for you. Please, allow me to escort you to where you can rest. I will have my father produce a draft, to aid in your sleep."

Thya stifled a yawn. "I am weary, but rest will not come until the last of our company has made themselves known."

"I must insist," Valcan pressed. "A chamber has been prepared. I will not permit you to depart at first light if you are not well rested."

"Very well," she said, and took Somal's offered arm.

"Tsinians, heed me," she called. Somal unhooked his arm and stepped back. "There still one among you that has been named and not put themselves forward. Tis that you do not deem yourself worthy for this quest? Understand this. Tis the Changlins that summon the worthy and only they contain knowledge of what the Tsinian's purpose is on this journey. Come forth, it could be that you are the chosen one that could decide the fate of us all."

Somal remained at her side as more volunteers stepped forward and were turned away. She took his offered arm and they left the cavern, walking through another arched tunnel, then turning a corner to see a row of wooden doors. Somal steered her past the doors and signalled to a small entrance between two cave walls. She entered the space and was surprised to see a well-lit cave. A bed had been carved from stone and mounds of knitted quilts, pelts, and a mixture of colourful material covered the hardness of the bed. A blue silk gown with silver trim hung from a hook that had been drilled into the rock wall. She caressed the material and imagined the group of talented seamstresses that had made the gown for her journey. The fabric was light and looked silky.

"Somal."

"My lady," he said. "Do you require assistance? Forgive me, I will get your attendant."

"Nay," she called, "Come forth."

Somal stepped inside and looked around the cave, as though it was the first time he'd seen it. He bowed his head. "I am at your service."

"Inform me, how long has this chamber been waiting for my arrival?" She imagined the Tsinians chiselling away, preparing the chamber while the feast was happening.

"When we first entered Celdor caves, there was but three caverns: the largest, where we took nourishment; the Plecky – the cave where the sacred Changlins are, and—"

Thya held her hand up to stop him. "You are utilizing the titles of our structures in Tsinia?"

"With certainty. Celdor is our home. I understand you are accustomed to better. We hope you will forgive the bareness of your chamber."

"Nonsense," she said. "I'm amazed at what you have created. A lot of labour went into this. You are correct in your statement, this is a home."

Somal grinned.

She sighed deeply. "Alas, at what duration did it take to complete? When did you depart from Tsinia?"

"When we discovered the Warlord was gone there was panic at first, though we attempted to exist as if naught had changed."

But everything had changed.

"Omad insisted that we keep a record of the first day we were forced to flee Tsinia. Pertius is familiar with Earth's days and 'monts'."

"Months," she corrected.

"I do wish I had been taught some of how you existed on Earth…"

"I will teach you," she interrupted. "Good, Somal, do continue."

"I took it upon myself to inquire with Pertius of the duration. Celdor Cavern has been our home for two years and seven months."

"Oh no!" she cried. She sat on the edge of the bed

and stared at the grey flint wall. "If I had remained this would never have occurred. Why was I not sent for immediately?"

Somal swallowed. "My father spoke of how distressed you were before you left. Everyone knew of your disdain for Tsinia."

Thya sat up straight and laid her hands in her lap. "You are mistaken. Tsinia is my home and I hold all of you dear in my heart. Tis the memories – bitter memories – that I did not want to relive."

"I realize now. Your return has brought tragic memories to the surface. Allow me to fetch a draft to aid you in your comfort."

"Certainly, that would do well." She forced a smile as he left. Thya sighed, glad to have a moment of solitude.

She laid on the pelts and released the tears she had held back for so long. "Oh, Alkazar, I wish you were here."

After taking the draft Somal brought her, she undressed and folded Haty's clothes, leaving them in a pile on the end of her bed. Wearing just underwear, she slipped under a satin quilt. The draft made her sleepy and calm. However, she could not completely relax. She was too anxious about what the light would bring and where this quest would take her. How was she supposed to locate the Darkeye once they reached the city of Helkon, if they made it that far? And what then? She didn't know how to employ the Darkeye, so how was she to defeat Kovon? There was so much danger, so much uncertainty. A timid voice interrupted her thoughts.

Someone was outside.

She pulled on the pelt and covered as much skin as she could, before calling for Somal to enter. Only it wasn't Somal. A Tsinian wearing a green tunic stepped in and bowed low to the floor.

"My lady, I regret the lateness of my intrusion. Truthfully, tis been some duration to obtain courage enough to approach you." His head still bent low.

The Tsinian was thin and gaunt and resembled one with much worries and woes. She recognized his face but did not know his name. He refused to meet her eyes, which worried her. What was he hiding?

"Continue," she instructed.

"I do not reckon to be the chosen one; however, I believe I could be of assistance in your travels."

"How so?"

"I retain awareness of the Outlands; I would willingly be your guide. I am at your command and will bestow my labour."

"Come closer."

Thya waited until he stood beside her and then threw one of the quilts on to the floor and motioned for him to sit. He sat crossed legged, trying to keep his attention fixed on anything but her. There is something to be wary about when a person can't look you in the eye. She knew he was hiding something.

"I was led to understand there was none with this comprehension. I agree it would be beneficial to include you as one of the company. Alas, as I remarked previously, tis not my pronouncement. Declare to me, what are you named?"

"My lady, I am Icas, son of Hung from the

generation of Wecst. I possess not powers and can only offer my understanding and strength. I do not do this lightly, for I believe tis my destiny and my duty."

Thya sunk back into bed. "Icas, I am grateful that you came forward, for you release a huge weight from me. Your awareness is required on this quest. You are the final Tsinian to be named. Present yourself to Omad. It is his wish to know you. It matters not the lateness."

She smiled. "Icas, look at me."

There were too many lines for one so young, and his eyes were dull and contained no spark. He looked tired, and troubled, and Thya was determined to discover what haunted him. "I believe the four of us will succeed in this task and I am content with the choice of the Changlins. Go. Rest, for we depart early light. Receiving you as a guide has eased my mind."

"I am relieved that I am permitted to accompany you on this quest." He smiled before looking down at his feet. "I believe I would have followed whether I was needed or not. I pray to the Changlins that there comes an opportunity to demonstrate my worthiness to you. Rest easy, my lady." He bowed, then left.

A leader, a guide, and a healer. Thya doubted she could have chosen better herself. She fell asleep and awoke the next light feeling refreshed and in good spirits - until she remembered where she was and why.

Though she understood the urgency in rising, she didn't know how long it would be until she felt this warm and comfortable again. She knew they were in for a rough time. While she rested a few minutes longer, she contemplated her dilemma. Once again, she was singled out for a task, and it had increased in difficulty from her former duty. If she failed, not only would her kinsmen suffer, but all who resided in Enumac would be in peril. She wondered if other Ganties had as much strife. How would the former rulers have acted in her position? Did she retain enough strength to succeed? So much depended on her. Tis not good to dwell on what may be, my thoughts ought to be on my kinsmen's plight. They long for their princess, their saviour.

Thya was the last to rise. Her companions were outside, ready to depart, but Icas looked tired. He stifled a yawn and she couldn't help but wonder if he had the stamina for the journey. She needed to trust that the Changlins knew what they were doing.

After a brief conversation with, Zarc, she addressed her kinsmen.

"My loyal subjects, citizens of Tsinia, which will again become your land …"

Cheers rang out.

"Your princess and guardian of the Changlins bestows this pledge, that I will employ my power and strength in retrieving the Darkeye's twin. Then, my kinsmen, Kovon will suffer and, on this occasion, I will not be merciful. This is my oath to you all. I do not comprehend the duration of the quest; we could be absent for many Tril moons. Though Kovon has not yet learnt where you exist, I fear he will soon enough. Be prepared to defend yourselves and to delay as long as possible. I will not tarry and will return as soon as I am able. My thoughts and love remain with you."

Calls of farewell and good fortune followed them as they started the slow trek back down the mountain.

Omad, Icas, and Somal were loaded with supplies. She was not permitted to bear any weight no matter how much she argued. Omad had been chosen to carry the sacred stones. They couldn't leave them at the caves in case Kovon attacked. It was safer to take the Changlins with them. Her companions were clothed in lightweight garments that were dull in colour, so they would blend into the environment.

When they reached the bottom, she gathered them together and informed them on the route they must take. Icas was asked to lead them.

"I declare to you that with hope, valour, and strength, we will succeed, and I pray to the Changlins that we four will return to Celdor Cavern victorious."

The group stood in a circle around her.

"I remark for all," said Omad, "that you retain our loyalty, service, and love. We will surrender entirely to this plight and assist you by any means possible."

The three of them placed a hand on their breasts in a salute of loyalty.

***

The trek to the forest took about three hours, but the flat terrain was easy on their legs. Thya was further aided by a staff Pertius, the tutor of the Tsinian code, had given her before their departure. Their path led into a wide expanse of dense, dark green, bushy trees. Omad shivered, and Somal and Icas looked at one another. Thya felt apprehensive and yet she couldn't understand why. It was if something waited for her. The dread of foreboding made her skin creep.

"I believe tis prudent we do not stray from this path. Remain collectively and be silent and alert."

"As you command," they answered.

They entered the forest at a slow, cautious pace. It looked harmless enough. Rays of broken sunlight lit their path. Icas led the procession; Somal followed, then Thya, and last was Omad. The trek was easy enough and uneventful. Thya puzzled over why she had been so fearful about entering but, as she started to relax, a fire sprang from the ground before them. The flames leapt and licked at them, blocking their way. They stepped back from the heat. The only way around the blaze was to deviate from the narrow path.

"There is something unnatural about these flames," she said. "Tis the Forest of Illusions, is it not?"

Omad nodded as he walked towards the inferno. He stretched his hand towards the angry flames. His scream pierced through the silence of the forest as his hand was consumed by fire. He yanked his hand away and clutched it to his chest. Somal ran to his aid, covered Omad's burnt and blistered hand with his own, and began the process of healing.

"Tis not an illusion, my lady," Icas cried. "We are compelled to proceed around the inferno."

"Nay, Icas, the forest is tempting us to stray from the path and I will not concede to its will."

Thya approached the flames and held her hand towards it. "Tis an illusion," she called out. "The flames are false. The heat you suffer is false."

"And Omad's hand, is that an illusion?" Icas dared to ask.

Ignoring his comment, she walked closer to the

flame.

"I am Thya, Princess of Tsinia, guardian of the Changlins, I will pass, and you will not hinder my way."

The fire soared higher, proving the fire was nothing more than an illusion.

"Nay, my lady, tis folly," Omad cried.

Thya stepped closer to the flames. As she reached for the burning inferno, she repeated in her head: *the flames are not genuine*, then plunged her hand inside.

Icas cried out as she stepped into the fiery blaze. She felt no burning. In fact, there was no heat. The flames licking her skin were cold to the touch. They flickered blue, then died down before vanishing completely. She sighed with relief as her companions ran over to her.

"You are unhurt?" Somal asked.

"I am unharmed. How does Omad fair?"

Omad held his hand out for her to inspect. Thya looked at the hand and turned it over. There was no burn mark or scar to be seen.

Thya smiled. "You are a skilled healer, Somal."

"How were you certain?" Omad asked.

"Why was Omad harmed yet you, my lady, were not?" Somal asked.

"If you had approached the blaze, full of certainty that it was an illusion, then you, Omad, would have come away unscathed. Complete faith was required. Come, let us not tarry. We ought to continue; precious duration has passed. Stay alert. There are foul things around."

They continued onwards. Their senses were alert, and their eyes sharp, not knowing what they would come across next.

There was no sign of the end of the forest and the branches cloaked the sunlight that had once lit their way. In the first instance of darkness, Thya heard a familiar but chilling voice calling to her.

"Thya. Thya, tis Alkazar."

She turned towards the trees and stared into the darkness, her heart pounding. "Alkazar? Where are you?" She ran to the edge of the path, pushing foliage aside as she entered the thicket, but something held her back, keeping her from reaching Alkazar. "Release me!"

"My lady, do not stray from the path," Omad called, grasping her arms.

Thya shook herself free and rushed into the forest, following the sound of his fading voice. "Nay, do not depart, Alkazar."

A light materialized and Alkazar appeared before her, dressed as she last remembered him. He held his hand towards her, silently begging her to join him.

Thya dropped to her knees. *It is Alkazar. My love has returned.*

"Thya, my love, approach me. I yearn to retain you in my arms."

Tears of joy rolled down her face. Somehow, he had come from the great beyond and was standing in front of her. He wanted her to go with him. And she would have given anything for this to have happened when Enumac wasn't in danger. When so many didn't depend on her. She couldn't be selfish. She had to put the needs of others before her own happiness. The light faded and Alkazar stood before her, whole. His arms opened. She so wanted to be wrapped in them, just one more time and, when he bent down and offered his hand, she reached for it. She was afraid their connection would make him disappear but as their fingers touched, electricity tingled through her body. His skin was soft and his hand firm. He pulled her off the ground and she stepped forward to embrace him.

Someone slammed into her side, pushing her away from him, and knocking her to the ground. Even before Alkazar vanished, she knew she had lost her chance. She cried into the forest debris. He had been an illusion, created by her desperation to see him once more. To say the goodbye, she had been denied. She knew she would never see Alkazar again. All the hope, love, and joy she had felt left her body, leaving her feeling tired and weak. She wanted to lay down and weep, but her companions would have none of that.

Icas helped her up and pointed to where Alkazar had stood. "My lady, look there!"

"Absolve me for my actions," Somal begged.

Thya couldn't answer. Her eyes were fixed on the pool of quicksand that would have pulled her under and choked her of air.

"My lady, you are well? Are you harmed?" Omad asked.

"How could I be so dense? It was an illusion and I fell so easily into its snare. I curse this forest," she yelled. "It feeds on our fears and emotions; the sooner we depart the better."

They returned to the path and continued walking. The branches were kind once more and allowed rays of light to show their way onward.

"Alkazar is dead," she said. "He will never return

to me. I understand this, and yet I was so convinced … What a fool I am."

"Somal was the only one who saw the illusion for what it was," Omad said.

"Then I am in your debt, Somal."

He blushed. "Nay, my lady, you owe me naught. 'Tis my duty to protect you."

She turned her head and looked back at Icas, who was walking with his head down, mumbling.

They continued in silence, until finally they saw the end of the forest and quickened their pace. It would be a relief for them all to breathe fresh air and leave the danger behind.

As they finally left the cursed forest, they were met with a thick growth of bushes. A path veered left and right. Thya studied the two roads. She had assumed that, by the time they had reached the crossroad, the Changlins would have informed her on which route to take, only no way had been made clear to her. When asked, Icas bowed and shook his head.

Thinking she would be clever, she ignored the two paths and pushed her way through the thick bushes, curious as to what lay ahead.

THE JOURNEY OF ICAS

Thya smelt the swamp before she saw it. Not being put off, she pushed her way through the last of the bushes and surveyed the scene. "The Changlins remarked of two paths yet crossing here will shorten our trek."

She wasn't certain how much time they would save, only that by crossing here, the mountain range of Klon would soon be in sight.

Thya prodded the thick green water with her staff. Bubbles rose and popped, emitting a pungent stench. Somal retched, and Omad coughed violently, then turned his head away. Icas' face turned a shade of green. Thya covered her arm across her mouth, hoping she wouldn't breathe in too much of the stench, and lowered the staff into the swamp to test the depth. Her eyes watered as she held what was left of the tip. It still hadn't touched the bottom.

She moved some distance away from the swamp before daring to open her mouth. "I believe it would be prudent to continue on another path."

The others nodded and then walked briskly to the crossroads.

Thya stared at the two pathways again, still unsure about which road to take. "We will camp nearby, and at early light, I will inform you of my decision. Go rest. I believe tomorrow will be eventful and tiring.

"Nay, my lady, tis you who require mindful rest and relaxation," Somal said. "How else are you to understand the correct route to follow? Icas can aid but a little with his knowledge. You, my Lady, have a connection to the Changlins and we are certain when you require their guidance, they will aid you. Do you desire to converse with them in solitude?"

Thya shook her head and smiled tightly.

They lit a fire and set up wards to protect the camp. Icas took the first watch while the rest of them laid close to the flames. Nightmares plagued Thya's sleep, with one of the dreams being so vivid it must surely be a warning.

Two roads. One would lead to certain death, but which was the correct one to take?

She gave up trying to sleep and pulled the cloak to her chin with a shiver. The fire had died down. There was no crackle, no orange glow, and no heat. She stared into pitch darkness. Nothing moved. It was as though all her senses had been blocked. It felt unnatural, eerie, but then Thya remembered where she was and how normal it probably was. She was about to chuckle at her sudden relief, when the silence was broken by whispers from Omad and Somal. Thya strained to listen.

"I pity the princess, that one so young retains much responsibility," Somal said.

"Unfortunately, the responsibility comes with her title," Omad replied.

Someone stood up, snapping a stick beneath their weight. Thya sighed, grateful for a familiar sound.

"Certainly. Alas, it was not her choosing. All that she has experienced here, I believe none other could endure."

"Tis so," Omad said, "She has a strength unlike any other. A will stronger than we could ever imagine. Yet, tis her duty to aid her kinsmen. Whether the princess agrees with this or not, she has accepted her role, as every Ganty ought to."

"And yet she is not like another," Somal argued. "So, it is alleged."

"I fail to remember you have yet to witness her remarkable gifts. I am certain you will shortly. Tis because of her uniqueness that she ought to be carefully guarded. Even Thya does not comprehend the extraordinary power she possesses."

Their voices fell silent. Thya focused on returning to sleep but ended up tossing and turning. Every time she closed her eyes, she saw Kovon with soldiers that didn't look human. The vision was blurry, but she could make out enough to see the strange creatures pointing spears at her.

A cool hand touched her forehead, and she remembered no more.

***

Given how disturbing her rest had begun, she was surprised to wake feeling rested and in good spirits.

Sitting up, she stretched and turned to see the others busying themselves. Icas was spreading out the ash of the dead fire. Somal was packing up their bedding, whilst Omad was preparing breakfast.

"Did you rest well, my lady?" Somal asked.

"Verily," she replied. "Tis your doing, I'm sure."

She stood up and brushed dust from her cloak before tying it around her shoulders and walking over to Omad.

"Nay, my friend. We ought to conserve our food for we do not know our duration here."

Omad nodded and started to repack.

"Remove the pastry," Thya said as she touched his shoulder. "Store it well. The fruit will be sufficient."

"You are decisive on which route we will proceed on, my lady?" Omad asked as he handed her the sliced peaches Grenko had grown.

No, she had not decided, and yet she couldn't tell them that. They were placing their fate in her hands and she had sworn to them that, at the arrival of the crossroads, she would know which way to go. They depended on her, yet her dream had deepened her anxiety, more so as it was the Changlins that spoke through her dreams.

What was certain was that one path would lead to certain death, but which one?

After an inner voice gave her information and instructions, she was still left to make her own decision - whether it was the correct one or not.

"I believe the left path will direct us to Lake Weir, this I am sure on. The right path is named the Path of The Unknown. I do not desire to journey on an unknown path. At least we are aware of where the other leads."

"Very well, my lady, if tis your decision, so be it," Omad said.

The choice had been made without a second thought. She hoped it was a good sign.

"Many have expired whilst attempting to cross the lake," Icas spoke out.

He had been silent throughout the journey so far, and Thya was surprised to hear him speak.

"'Tis believed that creatures named Grifiths exist in the lake."

Somal raised his eyebrows. "What is a Grifiths?"

"Water Demons. Cruel, vicious little monsters, or so I am informed." Icas looked away.

Omad stared at the road ahead and then looked at Thya. The prospect of meeting such creatures, if they existed, chilled Thya, but she refused to show any fear. Her resolve was set, and she stood up straight and spoke with as much conviction as she could manage. "At least we are aquatinted with what we are to face. We do not hold an understanding to where the Path of The Unknown will take us. Indeed, I am satisfied with my choice."

No one agreed.

The path was uneven and littered with sharp grey rocks, making the trek slow and difficult. It was as though the path was trying to stop them from reaching Lake Weir. It seemed never ending and, after several hours, the path narrowed, and the trees seemed to close in around them. Soon the way ahead became so dark, Thya could hardly see the path. Woodland surrounded either side of the road, yet it was the strange silence that caused her to shiver.

"Do not stray from the path, and remain alert," she called. "I fear we are not alone."

"The air is oppressive," Somal said. "'Tis as though the forest is waiting, yet the stillness is as if naught dwells within."

"There is a presence," Thya whispered. "There are eyes watching."

"We are being tracked," Icas said.

A rustle in a nearby tree caused Thya to stop walking. Somal turned his head from left to right, searching. Omad and Icas stood in front of her with their staffs held out. An immense dread flowed through Thya. Something was stalking them and, because she didn't know what or who the foe was, she couldn't prepare for an attack.

There was only one course of action. "Run," she yelled. "Run as swiftly as 'tis possible."

As they made their escape, the cause of her dread revealed itself as bright red laser-like eyes. Hundreds of them dotted the blackness and thick bush growth.

They ran as fast as they could. *If we can find daylight again, we will be safe.* Remaining in the darkness would be the death of them, Thya knew.

Something pierced her arm, not unlike a bee sting, but she ignored the ache and continued running. Her companions pounded the ground behind her and, in the distance, a sliver of light twinkled in the darkness. "Praise to the Changlins," she whispered.

Thya stumbled as her stomach twisted. Her vision blurred, and she shivered as a chill shrouded her. One of her companions steadied her and, despite feeling like she was dying, she pushed forward. They had to reach the exit.

"With haste," she called.

The trees seemed to part, and glorious light shone on the widening path. They left the darkness and chilling red eyes behind them and feasted their sight on the lush green valley head. Lake Weir glistened in the distance and would be at least another two hours of hard trek. Thya breathed in the fresh clear air. She had never been so grateful for light before. Only now the fear had left her, goose bumps chilled her skin, as though she was being frozen from the ground up. She forced her drooping eyes to stay open and turned to the others. They were hot and sweaty and out of breath, but otherwise unhurt.

"Are you well, my lady?" Omad asked.

She nodded. "I assume I chose the wrong route." She managed a weak smile. "We will rest and recover our strength."

Somal gasped for breath. "What were … those things?"

"I am not familiar," Omad answered, "and I am happy we departed before we discovered what those eyes belonged to."

Thya cursed herself for leading her companions into danger. Her teeth chattered, and her body shook as she shrugged off her cloak and placed it on the ground. She curled into a tight ball and hoped the chill would disappear.

"My lady!"

It took a further three calls and a gentle nudge

before she found the strength to open her eyes. She hadn't intended to fall asleep, only to rest for a while.

"My pardon for waking you, only we are compelled to continue our journey, or at least arrive at Lake Weir prior to the light fading."

Thya blinked, but her vision was blurred, and her eyes stung. Her body felt stiff and heavy, and it took a minute or so before she was able to pull herself into a sitting position.

"I did not realize the lateness."

The simple movement of sitting up drained her energy. Omad helped her to her feet, only her legs wobbled, and she collapsed into his arms.

"Somal!" he shouted, "Our lady is ill and requires aid."

Omad laid her gently back down onto the cloak as Icas and Somal ran over.

Thya shivered. "I am so cold."

Omad squeezed her hand as Icas took off his cloak and laid it over her.

Somal kneeled before her and studied her face. He placed his hands over her eyes, and his brow wrinkled. "There is a fever upon her, though it is not natural. She is weak and struggling to control—" He pulled his hand away and glared at her. "What occurred on the path, my lady? Did anything make contact with you?"

She nodded her head slightly. "I assumed it was not of concern."

"Where were you hurt?" Somal asked.

"'Tis a nip. Naught to fret for."

"I will be the judge of that."

Goose pimples covered her arms, but she couldn't

rub them because she couldn't lift her arms. Her body felt as though it was encased in ice and it took all her strength to whisper, "Alkazar," before slipping into darkness.

***

Somal checked that Thya had breath and then examined her arm. The skin around the entrance wound was purple, with veins of black branching off and travelling up her arm and towards the shoulder. He placed his hands on the puncture, closed his eyes and squeezed.

"'Tis poison," he announced. "Already it has spread. Leave me!"

Omad and Icas walked away, unhurriedly and not distant. Enough to give Somal the solitude he needed to work. Whether he had the skill to save Thya remained to be seen. He was not as gifted as his father and had very little duration until the poison journeyed to her heart. His father had taught him the fundamentals of reconstruction and repair damage but having the knowledge didn't mean he was capable.

Somal turned to the others. "The poison has spread swiftly. Tis in her blood and working rapidly." He closed his eyes and whispered, "Changlins, bestow onto me the strength to deliver Thya from fatality. Tis imperative that she survives, for we cannot fail."

Omad placed the Changlins in a semi-circle, then he and Icas knelt in silent prayer.

Somal closed his eyes and muttered his father's name before beginning the healing process.

When he opened his eyes again, the Tril moon was

upon them. There was enough light for him to see Thya's chest rise and fall, and he was relieved to see her breathing was steady now. Although he wanted to give thanks to the Changlins, he was too weak to walk that far, and stumbled to his bedroll instead. Omad woke as Somal approached, and he rose and ran over to him, taking the weight off Somal's legs. Omad's movements arose Icas, and he, too, ran to Somal's side.

"Our lady is well," Somal said. "She rests now, as will I. Maintain watch and rouse me if she stirs."

***

Omad watched Somal until he was deep in sleep, then turned his attention to Thya. He thought about all the princess had endured and all that was still required from her. She appeared so fragile and yet there was a strength, a power that he doubted anyone could contend with. Alkazar had warned Omad that the power – her second will – was unnatural and to be wary of her. He doubted Alkazar was in the right frame of mind when he had spoken of this. Yes, Thya was wilful and knew her own mind, and she was powerful, but he could not envision the princess as dangerous.

Kovon had acquired Tsinia already and, with his army, his power was increasing. What duration until he located the Tsinians' shelter? Omad was certain he sought the power of the Changlins, as his father, Darthorn, had before him. If Kovon were to place his hands upon the sacred stones, all of Enumac would be lost.

He gazed at Thya once more. Why should one so

young and untainted carry such burdens upon her shoulders? And what if the quest failed? Nay, he would not surmise such outcome. Thya would succeed. He wanted to believe this, alas the probability was set against them. Already the quest had come upon perilous hazards. How many more until they reached the city of Helkon – if they made it? And what then? Would she rap upon the gates and request the Darkeye? Omad shook his head. If they were to arrive at the city, he was confident Thya would know how to proceed. He shivered. She would surrender all to aid her kinsmen or die in the attempt.

Light came, and still he watched the princess sleep. Somal approached, and Icas stirred from his sleep.

"Did you rest well?" Omad asked Somal.

"As well as I was able."

Somal bent down and placed his two hands over Thya's chest, before taking her poisoned arm and squeezing it tightly in his hand. He concentrated hard, and though Omad tried to read his expression, there was naught. Until he turned and smiled.

"Our lady is well. The poison has been countered and her arm is healing. She will presently awake and require food. It will be some duration until she regains strength. We should prepare a human sling to transport her. I deem tis prudent to maintain our travels rather than delay further. What is your thought, Omad?"

"I concur, my friend, tis prudent to continue. I bestow praise onto the Changlins for your gift in healing our lady. Consume, for you also require strength."

Omad took Icas with him to search for materials to make a large sling. Omad glanced up as his companion scrunched his eyebrows scrunched and pursed his lips. *Here resembles one with much woe*, he thought. When he voiced his thoughts, all he received for his inquiry was a shrug and further silence. The two worked diligently as they weaved dried grass to make a sturdy hammock. Two long and strong branches of thick wood were used to raise and keep the weight balanced correctly on both sides.

Thya stirred as they were packing and readying themselves for the journey.

She yawned loudly. "I believe I have slumbered for an eternity."

Omad smiled. "Nay, my lady, a short duration."

"Do you retain sickness?" Somal asked her.

"I am aware of hunger, as though I have not consumed for countless Tril moons."

Omad coughed and bit his lip. "It will be some duration prior to you regaining strength enough to travel unaided and we have delayed plenty. We will transport you across the lake."

He pointed to the makeshift sling they had made with dried grass and wood, then waited for what was to come.

"Nay, you will not!" she argued. "I will not have you bear me as though you were slaves. Nay! I will walk unaided."

Thya tried to stand but fell back down. Omad shook his head. Thya's outbursts and stubbornness were as legendary as her gifts.

Somal rushed over. "My lady, you are not yet adequate to travel. You do not retain strength enough for your legs to sustain your weight. I implore you to rest."

Nevertheless, she tried to stand again, as Omad knew she would.

Somal stepped forward and did the unthinkable. He pressed his fingertips to her temples, causing her to slump unconscious into his arms.

"What have you done?" Omad cried.

"The only act I could." Somal laid Thya gently onto the grass. "Our lady was being unreasonable. She will heal if she rests. I will wake her once we have crossed Lake Weir."

Icas stifled a laugh. "The princess will not be pleased when she awakes."

"I will accept whatever punishment she orders. I acted for her own well-being."

"I agree with you," Omad said, trying to calm the fear he saw in Somal's eyes. "Our lady is too important for this quest to fail and her stubbiness would be the failure. I have sighted this previously."

Omad's mind drifted back to the time when Thya first met with Kovon. Her temper and strong will almost cause the downfall of Tsinia. He shook his head into the present and silently scolded himself for daydreaming. "Let us waste not," he announced. "We will continue on. I deem tis prudent to cross the lake prior to darkness falling."

"Somal and I will transport Thya," Icas announced.

As they lifted her onto the sling, Somal glanced at her. He seemed nervous and Omad recalled that Somal was yet to sight her anger, though he was certain he must have perceived it from his father.

Icas slapped Somal on the shoulder. "Do not fret,

my friend. Thya will appreciate your action, and Omad and I will support you."

Somal forced a smile.

Omad led the escort into the valleys. They walked for over an hour before stopping to take refreshment.

"Ought we wake Thya?" Icas asked. "Tis much duration since the princess has partaken in nourishment."

Omad looked to Somal for the answer.

"I believe tis not prudent yet. My father bade me bring one of his concoctions. The juice will fulfil our lady's hunger. Nevertheless, I prefer that she remain in slumber pending our crossing of the lake. This, I leave to your declaration, Omad."

"I concur," Omad answered. "Perhaps it would be prudent to permit the princess further rest."

Icas' smirk didn't go unnoticed. He knew, as Omad did, the real reason for Somal's hesitation in waking Thya.

"My friends," Omad said, waking them from their daydreams "Lake Weir awaits. Let us not tarry."

***

Lake Weir looked more like a river than a lake. The black water rippled like thick cream and, although the breadth was the size of five staffs, the length appeared never ending.

"Tis possible to pass at this juncture?" Somal asked.

Omad nodded and smiled. "It seems unnecessary to walk further along. I will assess the depth."

He walked to the edge of the lake and stepped into

the cold black water. Reaching out with his staff, he stuck it as far into the lake as was possible. "I am certain the depth will increase as we cross. However, I doubt the depth will contact our breast."

Icas prepared to step into the water but stopped. He bent low and peered into it. Omad wondered what Icas had seen that he hadn't. Not a shadow could be seen in the unnaturally dark water.

"I will lead," Icas declared.

"Very well."

Icas stepped into the chilling water. Omad and Somal followed him, carrying the princess between them. The sense of danger increased with every step. No one knew where the next would lead. When Icas reached the middle of the stream he stopped and looked around.

"Icas, what ails you, my friend? Why do we stop? What do you see?" Omad feared something was wrong and searched for the cause of the fear. Something was watching them, of that he was certain.

Icas waded to the right.

"Where are you proceeding?" Omad shouted.

"Persist onwards," Icas called back. "Do not delay. Tis imperative you create haste." He moved further away and then stopped, turned and stared. He was treading water, then swam further out before swimming back to them.

Omad and Somal quickened their pace. The thick water slowed their progress and, with the extra burden carrying the princess over their heads, the bank appeared unreachable. What was supposed to be five staffs in length turned into ten and then fifteen. The end was in sight, and yet they came no closer. The more the distance appeared to grow, the faster Somal and Omad waded.

Omad turned often to look at Icas, who had stopped swimming to watch them. He wore a beaming smile on his face, yet Icas was a serious character, and rarely smiled. His expression alarmed Omad, until he caught a swift glimpse of small, green, and slimy looking creatures diving into the water from the bank – Griffiths – the mythological creatures rumoured to reside in Lake Weir. Each wide, cruel mouth spread from one side of the face to the other; extending their sharp incisors. Yet it was their piercing yellow eyes and black diamond-shaped pupils that would stay in Omad's mind.

Omad glanced between Icas and the awaiting bank, where at least a dozen more of the vicious creatures appeared.

The Griffiths on the bank stared at both Icas and Thya. Icas splashed the water and they looked back at him, gnashing their teeth before diving into the lake. Omad's insides twisted as Icas' smile faded. Omad wanted more than anything to save Icas, but he understood why he was surrendering his life. The survival of Enumac depended on Thya, and Icas had vowed he would give his to save hers.

Omad and Somal pressed on, harder and faster, finally breaking through the false barrier of progression.

When they reached the shore, they laid Thya on the ground and turned back to the lake. Icas was surrounded by dozens of the green creatures.

"Icas," Somal screamed, "swim away, I beg you."

Icas raised his hand out of the water but made no move to escape.

"If the princess discovers my betrayal," he shouted, "express to her that I paid for my defiance, though even the surrender of my being could never atone for the suffering I caused both herself and Alkazar. Absolve me—"

The Griffiths pounced on him, dragging him under the water with their sharp talons.

"Nay. Icas!" Somal screamed and ran forward.

Omad grabbed the sleeve of his tunic and held him back. "Somal, you cannot aid him. It is done."

Somal shook off his grip. "Why?"

Omad turned his head away. He looked at Thya, who was still asleep and unaware of what had occurred. "Somal, we are compelled to get Thya to safety."

Somal bent his head low before nodding and returning to where Thya slumbered.

Although wet, cold, and lacking in strength, they carted the sling as far away from the lake as they could manage. Only when they were certain they were far enough away from the danger did they fall to the ground, lost in their own private sorrow.

STORM IN THE SAND

"I will awaken the princess, Omad. Only I plead that you inform her on the dreadful affair."

"Tis how it ought to be," Omad answered. "Seek firewood and, once we retain a blaze, you can wake her."

As soon as the fire was burning, Somal laid the palm of his hand over Thya's eyes, held them for a moment then stepped away. Thya awoke, and Omad's mouth went dry. Somal smiled and Thya returned it. Omad forced a smile too, should Thya happen to look his way. And then, imagining how strange it might look, returned to his forlorn look. When Thya attempted to speak, Somal put a finger to her lips.

"Nay, my lady. Everything will become apparent once you partake of this draft. You lack strength and, until I deem you fit, you will neither converse nor stir. Am I understood?"

She nodded.

With Somal's aid, Thya sipped the draft. The

medicine seemed to work instantly. Her skin turned pink, and the rose of her cheeks bloomed. Omad could almost feel the energy flowing through her. She emptied the flask and sighed.

"Do I retain your consent to sit up?" she asked Somal.

"With certainty."

Omad had remained silent, allowing Somal to take the lead, only it was his duration to converse now. Thya looked around; he knew who she was searching for.

"Icas will not be sighted, my lady." Omad swallowed hard. "He was lost to us at Lake Weir."

"What? No! This cannot have transpired. Somal, Omad, come sit with me and declare openly what has occurred whilst I was upon unnatural sleep."

Somal looked down at the floor. "Pardon me, my lady. My actions were unforgivable."

"And performed with reason," she interrupted. "You are pardoned, Somal, and appreciated for your deed. Now sit and inform on Icas' fate."

She listened and gasped when Omad relayed how he was taken. And, although he did not go into detail about the Griffiths, it was some moments after he had finished that she found her voice.

"If I had heeded Somal's instruction, you would not have possessed the burden of bearing me across the lake, and I could have employed my gifts. All of us could have reached the bank."

"Do not dwell, my lady," Omad said. "Fate has dealt a cruel hand yet, as you previously remarked, each has been chosen for a purpose. It seems Icas was destined to surrender his existence to save yours. Even if you had employed your gift, I believe Icas would have perished."

Thya nodded. "I am grateful for your words, Omad. I have plentiful experience of how cruel fate can be."

Silence fell between them, until Somal coughed. "What puzzles me is Icas' final remark. How did he betray you?"

"I too am perplexed by this." Her eyes seemed to lose their shine, but then she smiled as though thinking of happier times in the past.

***

"Come, you both ought to rest. I will attend watch."

Somal tried to argue, only Thya cut him off. "I want no slumber. Tis my command and you will obey."

Though it was not spoken in jest, she smiled, nonetheless. Omad and Somal were not foolish enough to disobey her command.

Thya watched Somal as he slept. She was grateful to have his company. He was a gifted healer, like his father, and he knew how to take charge and put her in her place. She smiled at that thought. She needed that – someone who could handle her when she was being stubborn.

Alkazar had known how to handle her too.

She envisioned the scene in the forest during their first fight. She had just learnt about her arranged marriage to Kovon and had made it clear to the Tsinians that their fight wasn't hers. She had no intention of being anyone's saviour. She was selfish back then and had just wanted to return to normality. It never occurred to her that she didn't have much of a life. Everything so far had been a lie, as though her life was a play and she was the star. And now the performance had ended, it was time to take the costume and makeup off and get back to her real life – in Tsinia. She bit her lip as she recalled his sharp words.

"I did not pursue you out of pity," he told her. "You are selfish, Thya. You retain gifts and possess a power we can only dream of. Tis a precious gift. You retain the fortune to become a heroine, to rule our land, one that is rich and bountiful. Yet you are resolved to whine and feel regretful for yourself. Certainly, tis written that you are our hope, only I wonder if you serve the purpose."

She shook her head. Those memories of Alkazar were bitter.

Thya sat in silence and contemplated the present and what they had endured so far. What should her next action be? She tried to envision what lay ahead. The problem was that she had no clue. The journey had only just commenced, and she had already lost one companion. *Do I retain the capability to complete this quest?*

She watched the Tsinians sleep. Somal was so like his father and yet far too young to be placed in such peril. Omad. He was old in growth yet not in spirit. She should never have permitted them to accompany her on this quest, but the Changlins demanded it and, as she had been repeatedly reminded, each had a purpose. Somal's role had been made clear, and Icas', but she couldn't fathom what Omad's role was.

So many questions raced through her mind. She

watched the pink tinge of sky and the two moons, one crescent and the other full. No matter what the day brought, the morn would start on a positive note and her companions' hearts would be lightened.

As daylight appeared, she watched Somal and Omad waking.

"Did you rest well?" she asked.

"Verily," they both replied.

"And yourself, my lady? How do you fair?" Somal asked.

"I believe this coming day will bestow a revelation and happiness will pursue. Consume and ready yourselves for departure, we ought to continue."

"What is our destination?" Somal asked as he shook his bedding out then swung the cloak onto his shoulders.

"We will continue north and will presently sight Death Valley, a barren wasteland. What in my language, I would name a desert. Beyond that, we will arrive at the mountain range of Klon. Further is yet unknown to me. Our objective is to cross Death Valley prior to the light fading."

***

The journey was quick and made easier by the soft grassy terrain. Midday had not yet arrived when they reached their destination.

A desert of golden sand lay in front of them and it seemed to stretch for miles. There was no sign of vegetation or life and it looked endless. Somal swallowed hard as he looked at the sea of sand. Omad sighed, but then straightened, readying himself for the trek.

"My friends, the desert is not as big as it seems. The mountain range of Klon is not so distant," Thya assured them. Only she had no idea how long it would take to reach the mountains. She refused to inform the others about the terrifying vision she'd had, of Kovon and his armies attacking Celdor cavern. She took it as a warning of what would be, should she fail, and refused to wait until the heat abated before crossing the desert. There was nothing she could do for her kinsmen now except complete the quest. It was imperative they get to the city of Helkon and find the Darkeye.

"If this wasteland is likened to a desert, the mid of light will convey with it immense heat," she said. "Discard all baggage that is not required, bear only supplies and necessities. If we do not halt often, I hope to arrive at the mountain range of Klon ahead of the Tril moon."

Omad was adamant he was not going to abandon his cape, no matter how hot it became. Somal carried the only pack, which contained food and drink.

They had travelled for maybe thirty miles when Thya sensed danger, only there was no sign of a threat. "Stay aware, for I believe we retain company."

They looked around and waited – alert. The sand before them rose into a shape of a hill and moved towards them at such speed they had no time to prepare for it.

From about ten meters, whatever it was stopped and showed itself. Its head was all they could see at first, but even that was terrifying. It showed a circle of a hundred or so slimy, sharp teeth. As the creature snarled, slime dripped from one tooth onto another. Its head shook as it let out a high-pitched scream. Thya, Somal, and Omad fell to the sand with their hands pressed to their ears. When the screaming stopped, Thya stood up.

Initially, she thought it was just a huge, gaping mouth with razor-sharp teeth, but a single eyeball sprung from the back of the creature's throat. It stayed there, suspended between its mouth by a thin rope of flesh. The eyeball was bright red and had a black, sinister-looking iris. The solitary eye stared back at them. When the eye rotated, she saw what she assumed was the creature's tongue. It looked like a Venus flytrap.

She had never seen anything like it and, for a moment, was transfixed. Once she got over the initial shock, she stepped in front of Somal and Omad. Precious seconds had been lost, and she wasn't wasting any more.

"Retreat," she ordered in a tone that made it clear she expected to be obeyed. Omad and Somal did as she asked. She didn't turn to face the creature until she was sure they were far enough away.

Thya waited until the creature was almost upon her. Its slimy mouth opened wide, ready to chew her up, but she was going to give it something else to chew on. Lifting her hands, palms out and with her fingers pointing to the burning sun, two huge fireballs emerged from her fingertips. She aimed at its gaping mouth. The ball of flames propelled down the creature's throat and into its tunnelled belly. There, she lost sight of it.

The creature reacted with a deafening howl that shook the desert and beyond. Thya covered her ears as a glow appeared at the end of the creature's body and, very slowly, the skin began to crack and then disintegrate. The creature burned from the inside out. The howling turned to screaming as it twisted and struggled to control the pain and the blaze from within. The sight and smell sickened Thya, and she turned away. Somal cried out a warning and she turned to see the head of the sand monster explode. The Tsinians leapt to the ground and covered their heads with their hands.

Thya created an ice shield forty sheets thick to protect herself from the flaming debris. She came away unscathed but Somal wasn't so lucky. A horned spike had slashed his right arm, ripping the skin open.

Two more of the giant worms reared from the sand. While Omad aided Somal, Thya created another ice shield to protect them and then stepped out to face the creatures. She fired immediately, her aim directed at the creatures' gaping mouths. One ball of flame was enough. The creatures reacted in the same way as the first: deafening howls, followed by piercing screams, ending with horrendous explosions.

Thya stayed poised behind the translucent shield, bracing for another attack. Whether there were only three sandworms in the desert, or word had gotten back to the others that she was not to be messed with, remained to be seen, but there were no further attacks. Once she was certain the danger had passed, she ran over to Omad and Somal.

Both were seated on the ground. Somal held his injured arm to his chest, his face taut with agony. Omad had done his best, ripping his beloved cape to tie three sashes along Somal's arm. The pressure stopped the bleeding, but the sunken brown sand showed that he had lost too much blood.

"Can you not heal yourself?" she asked.

"Nay, my lady."

"Healers only retain the power to heal others," Omad said, "and he cannot advise me as I do not possess healing gifts."

"Nay." She sat on the ground beside them. "There has to be another outcome. Inform me of what is to be done and I will heal you. Does it pain you much?" she asked, though it was obvious by the grim expression on his face that it hurt him. "Is there remainder of Valcan's draught?"

"Alas, my lady, there is naught," Omad answered.

Of course, there wasn't. She remembered drinking the last drop after her unnatural sleep and blamed herself for Somal's pain.

"Is there naught further we can perform?" she asked.

Somal shook his head, too distressed to speak.

Thya stood up and put her hands on her hips. "Then you will return to Celdor cavern, so your father can heal you. Only when he deems you fit to travel will you return to me. I am still in requirement of my healer." She ended the order with a smile.

"Omad," she continued, "you will accompany Somal and aid him in his journey."

"Nay, my lady," he argued, "tis not prudent to abandon you, regardless the duration. I agree that Somal requires aid. Perhaps we will locate aid whilst on our travel?"

"I refuse to permit Somal to travel unaided. I order you to depart, Omad. Already we have lost Icas. I will not lose another. You are familiar with the return journey and perhaps you will encounter aid along the way. We have covered much of this wasteland. I have little further to travel."

Omad shook his head and stood up. "You are in error, my lady, and I will not abandon you. I feel there is much desert yet to travel. In cause of this, I demand that I continue as your escort. I can be employed as a decoy ought the requirement arise."

Thya recoiled from his words. "I would *never* consent to this. Omad, how could you perceive this?" She closed her eyes and sighed. "We have delayed much, and I will continue alone. Somal requires aid and you will be of service to him. This is my command, and it will be obeyed."

Omad opened his mouth to argue when Somal sighed and said, "Although I am unable to travel well, I concur with Omad that you, my lady, ought not to proceed without escort. I fear you will face numerous perils and there is still some distance prior to reaching the city of Helkon."

Thya looked down at him and scowled. "You deem that I cannot mind myself? You are not familiar with me, Somal, and I do not retain the duration to prove my worth to you. Omad will confirm that I am well able for defence."

"'Tis not my desire to offend, my lady, I merely wanted to convey the dangers. I am aware of your gifts."

"Permit me to continue with you," Omad implored.

"However," Somal broke in, "the ultimate decision

is yours, Princess."

That settled it for Thya. She would continue alone, and Omad was going to find aid for Somal.

Somal gave Thya his cloak, which she tied into a sling to carry a full canister of juice and fruit - enough, she hoped, to last until she had crossed Death Valley.

She continued her journey with optimism and, although hindered by two more worm creatures, which she disposed of with ease, the trek was smooth, yet never-ending. After what seemed like hours, she rested and ate some of the fruit, which was spoiling in the heat. They had started the journey early, when the moons were still shadowed by Tsinian light. Only now it was well into midday. The heat was blazing, which would only make her trek more difficult. She had assumed to be out of the desert by now, especially as her flask was half-empty.

The hours trudged by; every step she took was made harder by the fine sand, piled into dunes. Her strength drained as she climbed and slipped down the mountains of sand.

The heat was unbearable. She was finding it difficult to breathe and her throat felt sore and dry. With reluctance, she drank the last of the of the quenching juice, convinced she didn't have much further to go and would soon sight the mountains of Klon.

Her optimism withered. She lost all sense of direction. For all she knew, she could be walking back the way she came.

To try to lighten her drowning spirits, she sang the Tsinian lullaby her mother had once sung to her, but it pulled her into despair as her thoughts went to Alex.

Oh, how she wanted to hold him and inhale his scent. She *would* succeed – if only to see him again. The thought of Alex waiting for her to come home pushed her forward.

Light faded and, although the heat cooled, the wind picked up and sheets of fine sand swept towards her. She tried to shelter her face from the stinging grains as all sense of hope faded.

"No wonder tis named Death Valley," she mumbled, surprised to hear her own voice and how it felt like company. It made her think of the people who were thought of as crazy because they talked to themselves, yet in their mind they were lonely and the voice, their voice, gave them company.

"If I had not been so pig-headed, we could have all crossed the desert and found aid for Somal. Why do I always get myself into these situations?

"Because you're stubborn," she answered herself.

Walking became difficult; her body felt weighted. Every step took strength that was quickly running out. Thya yawned and her eyes drooped. She shook her body and slapped her face, hoping it would wake her up.

"Tis not much further."

Her stubbornness won, and she continued walking and stumbling until she could not go any further. She stood hunched, defeated. Her legs crumbled beneath her and she rested on the cool, soft sand.

"It cannot conclude here." She cried dry tears. Although she wanted to crawl and drag herself across the sand if she could, her body refused to move.

Dehydration, sunstroke, and exhaustion had got the better of her. "I am sorry," she whispered. "I have failed you all."

She closed her eyes and was taken to a place free from heat and danger.

THE LONG-AWAITED REUNION

Janus leaned back on the old creaky chair looking around the sparseness of his cavern. The bed made of rock was softened by feather- stuffed duvets and was comfortable enough. His wooden desk needed replacing as did the matching chair. Both were basic in design but not comfortable enough to sit at for prolonged periods. As he stared at the cold, barren walls they morphed into the beautiful sitting room of his previous home nestled within the magnificent branches of the Tsinian trees. He inhaled deeply, remembering the wonderful fragrances the land held.

"Janus!" Galf called again.

Janus jumped and bit his lip. It had been a long time since he had thought of Tsinia and yet vision was as clear as if he was in the magical land.

He nodded to Galf and they clinked cups and drank sweet berry juice.

There was a sharp rap on the oval wooden door and then Calix, head of the Torpas guard, walked inside.

He stood silently in front of them. The chief nodded his head.

"Pardon the intrusion, Galf. I retain dispatch which will be of interest to you. Numerous messenger birds have been dispatched by the Tsinians. It seems the report is being conveyed across the Outlands and I fear enemies will discover what has passed. I communicated with the flock and discovered strange tidings."

Janus sighed as he waited for Calix to complete his report. The Torpas had a long-winded way of communicating, with much time passing for them to get their statement across, and he had little patience when it came to news from Tsinia.

"A travelling party of four Tsinians have been dispatched on a quest to locate a powerful crystal that dwells within the city of Helkon."

Janus stood up and rubbed his eyebrow. "That's Theon's domain."

Calix nodded. "'Tis remarked that only with the crystal and the power of the one that seeks it, can the warlord Kovon be conquered. Tsinians request aid from all who are willing to assist."

Janus wiped his palms on his tunic. "Do you retain the name of the crystal?"

"With certainty," Calix said, puffing out his chest, "'Tis named the Darkeye."

Janus sat back on the chair. It creaked under his weight. He swallowed hard. "Was it not destroyed by the Tsinian princess when she defeated the Warlord of Senx?"

"'Tis so," Galf answered, "And yet Kovon exists. Perchance the Darkeye was not destroyed."

"If tis so, why would the Darkeye be sighted within Helkon? Do you retain the names of the travellers?"

"Nay, this information was not relayed."

Janus patted Calix on the shoulder. "It matters not."

"I am grateful for the news, Calix," Galf said. "You may depart but be sure to visit if you discover more."

Calix nodded and left, shutting the door behind him.

"So, these Tsinians have been sent on a quest to locate a powerful crystal," Galf scoffed.

"Do you not believe it exists?"

"Oh, with certainty. If this news was relayed in cause of an oracle, then it is righteous. I believe they have an exceptional reader." Galf stared at him. "Ignore my words. I am an old warrior, envious that these doubtless powerful and young Tsinians have the opportunity to partake in such quests and battles. Oh, what I would do for such capabilities. Alas, I am aged now and should know better than to fantasize about what has long passed. I doubt they are having a pleasurable experience on this dangerous quest. What say you, Janus? Do we have Torpas able enough to locate and bestow aid to the travellers?"

"With certainty," Janus replied and stood up. "I will arrange an entourage of ten or more able Torpas to accompany me. I desire to discern more about this quest and bestow aid if need be."

Galf smiled.

"With your leave, I shall depart and make ready for the journey. I hope to discern where they have been last sighted."

Galf nodded. "Calix will aid you in that."

Janus nodded and turned to leave.

"Visit upon my cavern prior to your departure, Janus. I have something for you."

***

After Janus found and arranged with the few Torpas he discerned were suitable to accompany him on the journey, Janus found Calix at the edge of the woodland beside the Watcher's hut.

"What duration has passed since their quest commenced?" Janus asked. "Tis essential to know their location. How far have they progressed?"

Calix nodded and screeched into the trees. Several of the birds answered. It was Janus's first time witnessing the wonderful gift of Mynd being mastered by a male Bora.

"It could be some duration until we receive news, Janus."

"No matter, I will remain."

"May I fetch refreshments?"

"That is well done." Janus smiled and watched Calix run back up to the caves.

They had barely ended their lunch when the sleeping forest came alive with screeches and squawks from numerous birds. Janus jumped up and ran alongside the young messenger. No matter how eager he was to hear the report, he waited and listened.

"Four travellers departed from Celdor cavern and travelled through the Forest of Illusion and across Lake Weir…"

"Lake Weir? Why attempt to cross—"

"Sshh," Calix warned. "They are crossing Death Valley…"

They have travelled much then. He wondered how much time had passed since they had departed Celdor cavern. He silently tutted. They must require respite. It was foolish to cross Death Valley at light.

"Two remain," Calix said.

"Only two?"

What had befallen the others? It was tragic; nevertheless, the two that had survived would require assistance. "I am grateful for your aid, Calix."

Janus walked briskly towards the caves but stopped at the sound of insistent squawking. As he turned around, he saw Calix running towards him.

"There is further to report!"

Janus offered him water from his flask.

"Tis the queen," Calix panted. "The rightful queen of Tsinia is the one who seeks the Darkeye."

Janus grabbed Calix's shoulders and held back from shaking them. "Where is she?"

"Two are returning but need aid. The third continued through Death Valley and has lost her way."

"Her? The queen? The queen requires aid?"

"Tis so. I wait for further news."

Janus's stomach dropped, and his pulse raced. He turned to leave.

"The Queen," Calix called out. "You have encountered her?

"Tis so."

"I am told she is beautiful."

"Unlike another. You will sight her beauty when I return with her."

"Truly?" Calix's smile lit up his whole face before he turned and skipped his way back down to the forest.

Janus ran to the caves, ignoring the ache in his legs. Standing at Galf's door, he bent down to catch his breath before knocking loudly and walking inside. After Janus closed the door, Galf gestured for him to sit, only Janus was too agitated. He bounced from one foot to the other, too wired to stop moving. He wrung his hands as he paced and told the chief what had been discovered. Galf listened to Janus's excited recap and, when he finished, gestured for him to sit again. This time Janus complied.

Galf cleared his throat. "I may be an ancient Torpas, yet underneath these wrinkles you will locate a very astute individual."

Janus smiled as the chief poured Tamin juice into two beakers.

"'Tis naught my concern, and I realize you retain many secrets which you desire to remain hidden, only I deem there is more, save the quest that interests you? You would aid any Bora who required it, yet I fear there are other motives present. I sense that you are familiar with the queen. Perhaps you encountered one another on more than one occasion. Relate to me, that of her name?"

Janus's face lit up. His eyes shone and, for a moment, the worry lines creasing his forehead disappeared. "Thya," he answered.

Galf smiled. "Ah, certainly, Queen Thya."

Janus nodded. "She has earned the right to be named as such, though I am doubtful she accepted the crown. You are just in your thoughts. Thya and I have encountered on more than one occasion. She is highly valued by me." Janus held his breath and squeezed his hands tightly, yet inside, his stomach did somersaults. Only then did he feel an overwhelming sadness and squeezed his eyes closed, hoping his tears would not shed. The thought of seeing her, nay just perceiving her name, forced bitter memories to return. Yet he left Galf's room full of optimism and joy and met with the other Torpas who would accompany him to Death Valley.

***

Janus enjoyed walking through the Outlands, something he was never permitted to do in Tsinia. He especially enjoyed journeying across Death Valley. Alas, the sand dunes would hinder his progress and so, with Galf's consent, they opened the tunnels beneath the cavern. It was ancient and unused by the Torpas as they had been deemed them unsafe, but Janus was determined to make up for lost time.

One Torpas walked ahead of the others, lighting the ancient torches on the walls of the tunnel so the others could see ahead of them. Janus huffed with frustration every time they were forced to stop and clear sand and rubble where the inner walls had crumbled and blocked their path. The Torpas got to work quickly, throwing sand behind them and levelling it so it would not hinder their return. Although Janus concentrated on the job at hand, his thoughts were on Thya. She would be reaching the Devil's curve by now – if she had made it that far. It was the most difficult part of the desert to cross and he doubted her trek had been an easy one; the premonition that something was wrong drove Janus to push the Torpas to walk faster. When they reached the exit, Janus knew he had made a terrible mistake.

The tunnel was completely blocked. Janus's heart raced as he worried about how long it would take to clear the rubble and who knew how far along this avalanche of the tunnel was ahead.

Janus dug his hands into the sand heap, shovelling it to the side, while the others created a line and carried the larger pieces of the tunnel walls away from the cave-in.

"We must make haste." Janus urged.

He was internally cursing his decision to use the tunnel. The job seemed never ending when, as soon as it looked as though they were making progress, more sand would seep though. But Janus was not one to concede defeat. His throat felt dry and scratchy from the sand grains he'd inhaled. He violently coughed before being handed a skin-flask of water and then rinsing his mouth as he spat out the dust. He then noticed he was the only one not using his head dress as it should have been used. Mentally cursing himself he then covered his mouth.

Light seeped through a gap at the top of the tunnel. A sudden rush of energy surged through them and they scrambled through the sand, throwing it behind them until they were finally able to crawl out of the sinking hole. Janus helped the last Torpas to climb out. The sand filled the entrance, covering any trace that they were once there.

After a brief moment of rest to check the party were well and able to continue, they walked north.

Two silhouettes approached in the far distance. Janus shielded his eyes from the blazing midday light and looked again. There were just two, confirming that Thya was indeed missing. Janus ran as fast as the soft sand would allow. The Torpas gave chase but struggled to keep up. Janus didn't look back. His stomach fluttered at the sight of the old Tsinian. Omad was dressed in his usual brown robes and sported a long white beard still. Although his heart lightened at the sight of his old friend, he was anxious to learn news of Thya. He stood to catch his breath. Omad let go of his companion and stepped forward with his arms out in a calming gesture.

Janus smiled beneath his head dress as he realized how they must look to Omad, like a group of armed savages charging towards them. Even so, Omad showed no fear. Having reached Janus, he stood his ground, leaning on his staff and panting.

"My comrade..." Omad breathed out, then started again. "My comrade requires aid."

Janus held out a flask. Omad drank from it before offering it to his travelling companion.

"You will be presented with it," Janus answered, and then signalled to the other Torpas to help the other traveller. "Inform me, where is our lady?"

Omad straightened and bent his head to the side. His eyebrows rose. "She commanded me to locate aid for Somal. She continued the trek across Death Valley on her own."

"Typical," Janus said, and chuckled. He stared at

the younger, unfamiliar Tsinian.

"May I receive your name and title?" Omad asked, his gaze fixed solely on Janus.

"Do you not recognize me, old friend?" Janus said. He lowered the headdress from his nose and mouth and pulled the sandy material away from his head.

"Nay, it cannot be - Alkazar!" Omad covered his mouth with his hand and shook his head. "I will not question what good fortune brought you, only to reveal how relieved I am to lay sight upon you."

Omad stepped forward and pulled Alkazar to him. His arm rested on his shoulder and his hand patted his back.

"Dear, Omad, I beg of you, reveal to me how our lady fairs?"

"She is more gratuitous, more beautiful than ever and has taken the duty of ruler upon herself. You obtain knowledge of the quest?"

"Somewhat."

"Our Lady has again been set a huge burden; it seems she is forever acquiring the role of our saviour. Thya is our only hope, Alkazar, and not just for Tsinia. Kovon's forces will presently move. He has plans to dominate all Enumac and has the supremacy to do so. He is evil. Beyond all we could envision. He has returned with a heart for revenge and slaying, and he employs the dark arts. He is too powerful even for our princess. Tis why we require the Darkeye's twin. Tis the only method by which she can defeat him."

"I understand, Omad, and I lay a quantity of blame for the occurrence. We ought to have searched for him in Senx and not permitted him to escape. Alas, we were so inflated by his downfall that we did not understand the danger of his disappearance. I desire to aid Thya in her quest. Relate to me this instant - where did you separate?"

"We parted soon after Somal was hurt. It seemed the moment we stepped in to the Outlands our perils began. I did not desire her continuation. She insisted."

Janus smiled. "Fret not, I will locate Thya and escort her to the caves of Torpas. We can prepare for our continued journey there. Now, proceed in the company of the Torpas. They will tend to Somal's hurts."

Janus smiled at Somal, but it was not returned.

"Ought we to place our trust with him?" Somal asked, stepping back. "My father expressed love and respect for Alkazar, yet I learnt that he was a slayer of a woman and unborn child, and then escaped our justice."

"Hold your tongue!" Omad commanded angrily. "You are unaware what you remark."

"Nay, Omad, he has the privilege to opinionate." Janus looked long and hard at Somal. "You bear the similarities to a very gifted healer I knew. You are Valcan's son and so have the gift to heal? Understand this, I will transport your queen to safety and the Torpas will heal your wounds. You need not be troubled, the Torpas are harmless and honour my requests. You are protected within my care and, on my return, I shall demonstrate that I am to be trusted, only then will I reveal to you the true nature of my errors. Until that duration, Somal, proceed with Omad and be satisfied that you happened upon aid." Janus put an arm on Omad's shoulder. "Tis good to sight you, old friend.

We will converse on my return. There is much to update you on. For now, I depart in search of our lady."

"Be kind, Alkazar," Omad called out, "consider that she believes you deceased."

Alkazar nodded and smiled tightly before re-dressing his head and covering his face, then he turned and walked away.

THE AWAKENING

Alkazar ignored the heat burning the soles of his feet as he sprinted across the desert. The burning sand brought not pain though. Pain was not knowing if Thya was with breath. Pain was sighting her again of discomfort after this lengthy duration, after abandoning hope. He was conditioned to the harsh rays of the sun and the scorching of the sand. The headdress he now wore protected his mouth and eyes from the particles of sand in the air. He thought of the desert as freedom; far-reaching and empty, holding much promise and mystery. Only fate would know the route to take. However, he was not on one of his prolonged wanders. There was purpose to his journey. He increased his pace, anxious that even a second could mean he arrived too late.

Time lingered, but finally he saw a shadow in the distance. As he approached, it took the form of a figure – a figure on the ground. He prayed to the Changlins that she was still alive.

"Oh, you stubborn woman," he cursed. Although a Bora, she was all woman in his eyes. He watched her chest rise and fall, but her breath was jagged. The soft pink lips his mouth knew so well were dry, cracked and bleeding. Her milky smooth skin was red and blistered. She was breathing, but barely.

"Thya, my love." He took the carafe that was being offered to him from another Torpas and lifted it to her lips. She didn't wake, or even stir, and he doubted she knew he was there.

As Alkazar lifted her into his arms, the Torpas attempted to help. "Nay," he yelled and pulled her close to his chest.

He spoke softly to her as they retraced their steps. She felt than he remembered, and he wondered if she had been taking care of herself. "Oh, my love. You are home now Thya and I swear an oath I will protect you."

When they reached the entrance of the caves, the Torpas took her from him. He didn't cry out but silently followed them. Omad and Somal blamed themselves for her condition.

"My friend," Alkazar started. "I doubt any resolve would have satisfied our lady. Once the woman has her mind set naught can break her shield of stubbornness."

Somal smiled tightly and Omad nodded his head.

The Torpas took Thya to the healer's cavern. Somal made to follow but Alkazar grabbed his arm and pulled him back. "Permit the Torpas to heal your queen."

"I am the Tsinian healer and tis my duty and privilege to heal my princess."

"Tis so, Somal, yet you lack strength of your own." Alkazar placed his hands on Somal's shoulders. "I assure you their gift is as grand as your own. And I bestow to you my oath that, once they have completed their duty, only you will attend to her care."

Somal straightened up and nodded. Alkazar doubted this would satisfy him at length - his curiosity as a healer was piqued. Nevertheless, Alkazar was resolved to ban any Tsinian from entering until the Torpas had healed her.

He contemplated Thya's reaction on learning of his own existence.

***

"Omad, I hold concern for her mental stability when she discovers who I am. And yet, I refuse to delay our reunion. I need to hold and embrace my love. I am selfish in that respect."

Omad smiled. "I appreciate your want to have Thya back in your arms. And this will pass. Nevertheless, I agree that her mental health could be compromised on learning the truth. No matter how gentle the reveal is. I fear the shock could be too much. You asked for my council I hope you will take heed."

"I too have come to this conclusion. However, I doubt I have the strength to take a step back. How am I to be in close proximity and not embrace my love?"

Omad rested his hand on Alkazar's shoulder. "This will be a test of your resolve. Remember your pretence is for Thya's benefit. This alone should strengthen your determination."

The new visitors caused much excitement for the Torpas. Once it had calmed, Alkazar called a meeting of the Torpas and explained who their special guests were and that he intended his face to stay hidden from the princess. It was agreed that, while in the presence of Thya, he would continue to be addressed as Janus.

From the silent treatment and the glares Somal threw Alkazar, he knew that he had his work cut out for him to gain Somal's trust. But he was determined to prove himself a worthy friend, if Somal would let him.

After several healing sessions, and potions, Thya awoke, but she did not have the strength to stay awake for long periods. The days passed slowly, and Alkazar spent every waking moment at Thya's side. Never once did he remove his headdress or utter a word. He communicated through his hands, using mime, but was thankful that she would soon understand what he was trying to convey.

***

It didn't matter to Thya that her rescuer didn't speak. They had made a connection, somehow, and although it was strange it also felt special. The times they weren't talking, they spent walking. Even that was satisfying. Thya found him to be a kind, caring Torpas, and yet there was something else. A warmth, a love even, or maybe she was just imagining the signals in Janus's eyes. Maybe it was the sudden need for companionship stirring her emotions.

The next light after returning from their usual morning stroll, Janus gestured for her to sit before taking the sacred stones from his pack. He arranged the

Changlins around her and she felt the current flow through her. Their power, combined with her own, charged the atmosphere. Something significant was about to happen. Her heart raced as Janus knelt before her, took her hand and gently kissed it. Then he started to unwrap his headdress.

Thya's eyes were transfixed. She thought her heart was going to jump out of her chest. She shook her head vigorously. "No. It's not possible," she whispered. She reached out to touch his face, but her strength left her, and she slipped into darkness.

A soft hand caressed her cheek and her eyes fluttered open. And there he was. Alkazar, cradling her in his arms. Her Alkazar. How was this possible? Did she die in the desert? Was this all some beautiful dream that would come to a crashing end?

"Alkazar, tis truly you, or are you a miserable illusion?"

"Nay, my love, tis not an illusion. Oh, my sweet, how I desired to converse with you. Alas, your fatigue evaded me. I never believed I would sight upon you again. When I learned you were on Enumac, here, and located you in Death Valley, I believed I had lost you again. Oh, my love. There is much to convey. Where do I commence?"

"You will commence with an embrace." She laughed. "Prior to my wakening of this wonderful dream."

Alkazar pulled her close and kissed her. His lips were so soft and gentle, and moved in sync with hers. Butterflies fluttered below – butterflies she thought would never wake again. She could have kissed him for eternity, but a small, fake clearing of a throat separated their embrace.

A wide grin from Omad greeted them. "I am grateful the deception has concluded. So, confused am I with what to name you."

They all laughed and then Alkazar gestured for him to sit. "Come, be seated, Omad, for the tale I possess ought to be divulged in your presence."

Thya removed the stones, carefully putting them back inside the pack.

"Somal, too," Thya said. "He has become a valued friend, tis fitting that he be in attendance."

Omad bowed and left to search for Somal. Alkazar and Thya sat silently staring at each other. She could hardly believe that her heart, her soul, the only one who would ever make her feel whole, was sitting beside her. *How was it possible?*

She thought back to when the Tsinian council had informed her, while she was under an unnatural sleep, that by Alkazar's request, his execution had been carried out and his ashes scattered. Now, to save her sanity, she had to know why, where, and how?

Omad took around five minutes to find Somal. Thya instructed them to be seated, and then Alkazar began his explanation.

"Somal, you will endure with me as I will not back track. Perhaps you will discover how I came to be incarcerated; yet the duration is not now. My lady, I apologize for permitting you to believe in my demise. However, I have not regrets for my decision. After your departure from Tsinia, while waiting for my judgement, I was permitted solitude to curse my fate. As you all sight, fate had an unexpected turn.

"The true father of Siren's child liberated me. He was riddled with guilt and conveyed that he could not exist if he permitted my demise. He admitted he retained knowledge of Siren's plan from the onset and did naught to hinder the process. He begged me for absolution and desired the opportunity to repair the damage he had caused. He knew of the Outlands and informed me on how to get to welcomed shelter. He liberated me, and I can never repay him for that."

Omad looked at Somal and then they both looked at Thya. She nodded slightly and then bowed her head. "Alkazar, relay to me his name."

"Icas," he answered, "from the generation of Wecst."

Omad and Somal gasped, though Thya had already sensed the sad truth.

"You retain knowledge of this Tsinian?" Alkazar asked.

Thya told Alkazar that Icas was one of their companions and how he had lost his life at Lake Weir.

A moment's silence passed.

Omad coughed loudly. "My lady, absolve me for not conveying this to you previously, only I was mystified by his statement; even so, I memorized his declaration clearly. I relate to you the message bestowed to me by Icas prior to his untimely demise. 'If my princess discovers my betrayal, express to her that I paid for my defiance. Though even the surrender of my being could never atone for the suffering I caused to both her and Alkazar.'"

The words ended in silence.

"'Tis a noble sacrifice and Icas has my exoneration. He will be remembered as a martyr."

As there was nothing furthermore to say, Omad and Somal departed.

Once alone, Alkazar spoke to Thya.

"We ought to continue to Helkon for you delayed long."

"We?"

"Since I arrived at the caves of Torpas I have acquainted myself with the Outlands and you are familiar with my exceptional appetite for awareness." Thya laughed. "Well, I badgered the Torpas until they relented and disclosed all I desired. So, I am a connoisseur and the only one who can lead you safely to Helkon."

Thya was not convinced.

Alkazar laid a hand on her shoulder and looked into her face. "I understand why you insist on travelling such an unknown and dangerous path and I will travel with you."

"Nay, my love. I do not require your help, company maybe, but I will not leave anything to chance. I cannot lose you again."

"I am aware of how much Tsinia means to you and I will bestow my all to assist you in taking back your land."

"'Tis your land also."

He shook his head. "Nay, I am an outcast among my own. None know the truth and it must remain so." He closed his eyes and sighed. "I can never return to Tsinia." Alkazar took her into his arms. "Do not pity me for I am content, more so now that I have located you. The Torpas do not abide by rules of the lands and exist freely. Presently I am regarded, my talents and comprehension are respected, which is why they invited me to educate them."

Thya pulled away from him. Where were these words coming from?

"You have always been a leader," she said. "The Tsinians regard you in the highest esteem. You cannot deny this."

"Nay, I doubt it remains. Even so, I required more. I located what I desire among the Torpas and retain respect and standing. The Torpas permit me my studies and are attentive to my remarks. You are familiar with the sensation of suddenly being regarded and admired are you not?"

"'Tis an overwhelming sensation and I understand your reluctance to discard your new title and standing. However, you are Alkazar from the generation of Kapil, tutor of the arts in Tsinia and you ought never fail to remember this."

He laughed.

"How is this possible when you are present to remind me? Oh Thya, how I desire to hold you. To love you. To become one again, only I appreciate this cannot occur for the present."

She did not want to think about the future. Now was far more important.

"Your crusade is too valuable to delay further," he continued. "We ought to ready ourselves for the journey, even so I desire that you do not depart on such a perilous journey. There are evils around that you cannot imagine – for which you will require my aid. I believe you would persist unaccompanied. You are a stubborn Bora, Thya. However, I will not permit you to depart unless I am your escort."

She laughed. "You cannot detain me."

"This I can, and will, if the requirement arises."

"You would detain me?" She pulled away from him. "You would employ force?" She wanted to laugh at his suggestion but was too angry. "You would permit your fellow Tsinians to perish?"

"They are not my fellow Tsinians!"

"Do not utter such!" She covered her mouth. "Oh, how bitter you are. Do not forget you presented yourself freely to the council. You knew what the punishment would be and accepted this. You cannot fault them for obeying the code." She turned away from him and didn't realize she was crying until she felt his thumb brushing away her tears. He lifted her chin, so she had no other choice but to look at him.

"Oh, Thya, absolve me, my love. Tis not meant. I hope the Changlins curse me for my poisonous words. I have been absent from my residence for much duration and, as you state, I am bitter. Trust that I love my kinsmen, as I love you. I will continue with you on your crusade, not only as protection but to aid my kinsmen in regaining their land and name."

Thya looked into his eyes. Aqua blue, so mesmerizing. She felt like she could drown just staring. Her breath came out as a quiver and she knew she needed to pull away or her resolve would be lost.

She stepped back and brushed her dress as though it was dirty.

"Tis the love you retain for your latest kin, the

Torpas, that I demand you remain. You selected to be of their council and with this comes an obligation. You will not abandon them. You cannot accompany the princess of your past land. I understand why you will not step foot upon Tsinian soil - although I do not accept this. However, you, dear Alkazar, will accept your responsibility to your new kinsmen." She sighed. "The further the delay the bigger a threat Kovon becomes. Tis not only Tsinia I fight for, tis all of Enumac. If he is not hindered, he will develop into the master of all and I will not permit this to occur. The threat draws closer to your new dwelling, Janus. You will remain here and protect the Torpas."

Alkazar stood abruptly. Thya had known her decision would sting but would exert her authority as she saw fit. The stubborn Bora was not giving up.

"Do you not realize tis why I ought to aid you? By locating the Darkeye and defeating Kovon, I will be aiding the Torpas."

"And if you expire whilst attempting it?" She shook her head. Nothing was worth the risk of losing him again. It would kill her.

"The Torpas existed prior to my appearance and will continue to do so following my departure. Omad is a finer councillor than I could possibly be, he should remain until my return. He is not as agile as he formerly was. Why did you permit his journey?"

"It was not my decision, yet he has been invaluable."

"As am I, and I will not take no as an answer."

Thya laughed as tears formed in her eyes. "No! 'No' is not in your vocabulary. How are you familiar with such a remark?"

"You fail to remember that we once planned to return to Earth together. I studied your world and technique of speech. 'No' is the only word I could employ to display to you how determined I am to be your guide."

"Very well, Alkazar, I sense that you will not be put off, but respond to this. How will you be of aid to me? I am familiar with the route I ought to follow and will deal with any adversaries should they appear. You retain knowledge of how skilful I am. I do not require your aid, Alkazar. I am quite capable of looking after myself."

Alkazar stopped her there. "You present a funny way of displaying this. You contracted poison and nearly expired by travelling the wrong path. I located you almost breathless in Death Valley." He did not mention the loss of Icas. . "I concur your role has been adequate up till now." He joked.

Thya frowned as Alkazar continued. "From henceforth the trek becomes harder, more than you imagine. You will require all aid offered to you, if you are to succeed. Suppose you reach Helkon. What follows?"

"I understand your concern, and I admit, I sometimes choose in error. However, I learn from my errors and I am prepared to persist with the crusade. You did not respond to my inquiry. How are you to aid me? Pardon me, Alkazar, but you are merely a tutor of the arts and a concerned lover ..." She hated saying this but was running out of excuses.

He turned away and walked to the far side of the cave, leaning his head upon the cold, wet stone.

Thya walked over to him and touched his arm.

"Alkazar, I am regretful, but I address the truth. I understand your desire to assist, yet I believe it would be better for all if you were to remain."

Alkazar shook his head.

"What ails you? State your unease."

He turned, and Thya was shocked at how pale his face was. His eyes were no longer aqua but dull, almost lifeless.

"Thya, generations of Kapil were not tutors. I am the first such tutor. Kapils are known to retain the gift of Dispelling. Do you recall Jakar?"

Of course, she did. He had poisoned her confidant, gentle Kezar. She would never forget the pathetic appearance of the Senx.

Alkazar did not wait for her answer. "Do you recall Omad's words, 'A gift which you yourself are familiar with, Alkazar?' Well, I was familiar with it because I previously possessed the gift. I was capable of becoming invisible at will."

Thya gasped. "How can you mislay a gift like that?"

"I did not mislay the gift. It was removed." He turned to face her. "Do you also recall one of the council remarking that only the Changlins retained the power to eliminate such a gift and that I ought to retain knowledge of this?"

"Why would the Changlins remove such a gift?"

"I was a young Tsinian, by my second birth moon I was at the stage of learning my talents. I was the lone Tsinian with this gift and, even though the others retained their own, mine was looked upon with awe. I was a swift learner and began employing my gifts for my own leisure. What began as a prank evolved into something precarious. I gained a lot of admirers and many friends. I am certain that, if I had remained silent, I would have got away with it. However, I was young and reckless and enjoyed boasting about my amazing feats. Little duration passed before I was summoned to the Escos by your mother and father. I was accused of being the cause of all the strange disappearances from around the city. The Ganties ordered my gift to be removed."

I interrupted. "Surely your crime could not warrant such a drastic action? The Changlins would not permit this."

"The Changlins performed the removal. At that duration, I would have concurred with you. I did not comprehend the seriousness of my actions. Why did I deserve such penalty? Although, presently, I deem it just."

"Truly!" I gasped. "What did you execute that was so dreadful?"

"I employed my gift to steal possessions, without being noticed, and placed them elsewhere. It was amusing to sight older Tsinians searching for their missing pieces. I followed one of them into the Escos while he complained. Being aware that I could not be seen was such a thrill. I yearned for more. Eventually I attended every meeting. I heard things that a young Tsinian ought not to perceive. And of course, I couldn't maintain the intelligence to myself. I shared it with my newly-found friends. I did not comprehend the danger of my actions. I was willing to inform anyone who wanted to pay heed. I was stupid and reckless."

Alkazar fell silent. Thya did not know what to say.

This was a side of Alkazar she had never thought could exist.

"I remember standing in front of the thrones," he continued. "I was fearful. I speculated as to why I had been summoned. Still, it came as a surprise to have all my antics announced. Everything was revealed, including the disappearance of one of the Changlins."

"You did not!"

"Tis so. It was meant as a jest, only it was too difficult to replace the stone. Many guards had been stationed around and inside the Plecky. It caused such commotion, I ought to have realized the culpability would have been put on me. I was the only Tsinian talented enough to execute the act. I had got away with so much, for so long, I thought myself unstoppable."

He smiled briefly. "I was summoned into the Plecky alone. I understood what was to occur and I begged them to reconsider. I pledged to them that I would never misemploy my gift again." His voice became distant. "Beams of light emitted from the sacred stones, they entered me, and I screamed in terror at the occurrence, and the thought of not possessing friends, of being no one special, powerless. I was terrified of my future. I now consider tis why the Changlins removed me of such a gift. It was not my misemployment of it; I could only sight the employment of it for fun. I did not understand how unique and important my gift was. At that duration, I did not regard it as a gift.

"I became aware of a sudden coldness, as though ice had entered my veins. I felt the power drain out of me. It concluded within a matter of moments. Your parents were waiting outside the Plecky, they embraced me, and I broke down. I was so ashamed for what had transpired. I hid myself away in my dwelling, afraid to display my face. That is when I commenced my studies. I worked hard, for it seemed that was all that remained for me. Duration passed, and I was finally capable of educating others on how to control their gifts. That is when the Ganties announced that I was to be converted into the tutor of the arts. I suppose I located my calling. It was my way of proving how regretful I was. I was certain that not one Tsinian would misemploy their gifts and that from the age of learning they were taught how to respect the power that had been bestowed upon them."

"Oh, Alkazar," Thya cried and embraced him tightly.

"'Tis what the rulers demanded. The instance the gift was eliminated they decreed that my gift of Dispelling was never to be uttered again. Even so, I existed with the awareness of my shame and currently do."

"Yet you repaid for your foolish errors more than once. I am certain the Changlins would pardon you. Why would they not return your gift? You have appealed for the return of the gift, have you not?"

"Nay, ought I?"

"Oh, Alkazar. With certainty. You have earned the return of your gift. Why have you never related your desire to them?"

"I suppose I have not displayed an interest. Indeed, I believe I have avoided the Changlins out of fear of them. Recall the moon we spent in the Plecky together."

Thya smiled as she reminisced of the time they

consummated their love. After Alkazar was permitted to end his betrothal to Siren, they had made love for the first time inside the Plecky, believing it was just in doing so.

"That was my first visit to the Plecky since the elimination," he admitted.

"Oh, my love." She embraced him tightly. "Why did you not reveal this to me previously? It clarifies much."

Thya felt closer to him now that he had trusted her with his darkest secret. She cut off the embrace and looked him straight in the eyes.

"The Changlins removed your gift and I am certain they are able to return it. I will converse with them. I too possess the power to eliminate, though I doubt I can reinstate, otherwise I would not hesitate."

"And if my gift is returned and I possess the power of Dispelling, would you permit me to escort you to Helkon?"

"With certainty. A gift such as yours could be employed for several causes. I believe we are in requirement of your power to succeed and I am confident the Changlins will concur."

"Oh, Thya, if that was truly feasible it would be ideal. Do you desire for me to accompany? Ought we not visit the Changlins collectively?"

"Nay, Alkazar, you have not displayed an interest. Tis prudent that I perform this alone, for I deem some pleading will be required. Be patient, this could take some duration."

Thya left to find Omad, as he was the appointed keeper of the Changlins. He did not question why she wanted to speak with the sacred stones and handed them over. She walked some distance away from the caves to be alone and knelt before them.

When darkness fell, she knew Omar and Alkazar would be concerned so started walking back to the caves, paying little attention to anything around her. Her mind would not shut off. *What have I done?* Her chest tightened, and her heart raced. As quickly as the thought about having a panic attack, her heart regulated and the pain in her chest disappeared. She stood up straight and laughed. "No good crying over spilt milk." It was done and there was no going back.

As she neared the caves she heard Alkazar and Omad talking.

"She has been absent for much duration. I searched for our lady, but I cannot locate her. Tis not sensible to trek far unaccompanied, let alone with the Changlins."

"Fret not," Alkazar answered. "Thya will return when she is ready and, as for not being capable to mind herself, you ought to recognize better than to craft that judgement."

"With certainty. You are just, as always. Yet I do have concern. A great deal depends on our lady. She has come through for us previously, only currently she has the whole of Enumac to defend. Tis such a weight for one so young to burden."

"Only burden it I will," she answered.

Omad bowed as she reached the mouth of the cave, while Alkazar searched her face. Her eyes flickered to his and then down to the floor. He sensed bad tidings.

"Omad, leave us, for I desire to converse with Alkazar."

Again, Omad bowed, then went back inside the cave.

"I realize from the frown upon your face, my lady, that the battle was not won. The Changlins did not concur."

There wasn't much room outside the cave but Thya paced as she spoke while pulling at her fingers. "Alkazar, you ought not be punished for further duration and, as we come closer to war, the requirement for your gift grows stronger. Because of your lack of attendance and the avoidance of the Changlins, they are not assured. Tis not your trust, you have proven your loyalty to them and to your princess. I pleaded your case and the urgent requirement for the return of your power and I am certain they would have agreed. However, they took the opportunity whilst in this standoff, to compose an offer they were aware I would not refuse.

"Your gift will be returned and with it the gift of Illusor." Thya took a steady breath before continuing. "If I willingly accept the crown."

He gasped. "Nay, Thya, you will not. I will not permit you to sacrifice your freedom for me."

"Like you did for me."

Alkazar stared, opened mouthed.

Thya continued. "I learnt of your sacrifice, yet deep down I always retained belief that it was I that eliminated Siren. Well, another part of me, the one I have not yet learnt to control. What I have never been able to understand is why you received the blame, aware that you would forfeit your breath. I could never repay you. The nearest I can do is to return your gift."

Alkazar finally found his voice. "I would do it over again if I had to, princess." He stood up and walked over to her. "I will not permit this sacrifice. By taking the crown you can never return to Earth. You would be obligated to exist in Tsinia for the remainder of your duration and you would be miserable."

"I am aware of this."

"You would never be happy or content in Tsinia. I recall your longing for your home and in cause of this you refused the crown. Nay! I will not permit this."

"You cannot refrain me, Alkazar. Tis my decision alone. Oh, so much has changed. I believe it would be prudent if I resided permanently. Tsinia requires a ruler, a queen to shield and see that Tsinia grows bountiful and that her citizens are content and safe. I have not had duration to regard this, and yet it creates sense. My former journey to Tsinia brought me grief and danger and I will admit I was happy to sight the conclusion. However, I have located you again, though I never believed this could be possible, and even though hope hangs in the balance and we could fail, I feel more active, more hopeful, and more positive than ever. Tis where I belong. I finally understand that, and I am prepared to receive my rightful place amongst my kinsmen."

Tears threatened to burst from his eyes. Thya knew how long he had wanted to hear those words. She had allowed her emotions to run wild, yet it made sense. I have Alkazar. He is alive, and my love for him has not diminished. Oh, Alex, everything is just perfect. We can be a family. A fate I never dreamed could happen. How could I have known that my return would cause so much happiness?

"If you are certain?" Alkazar questioned.

"Certainly, which is why I accepted and taken my rightful position as the ruler of Tsinia."

Alkazar knelt before her and swallowed. "Queen Thya, again I bestow my oath, obedience, love, and trust."

Thya smiled down at him. "And again, I accept and will hold you to your oath, Alkazar, son of Kapil."

Alkazar stood up and gazed lovingly at her.

"Although there will not be an official ceremony until our arrival in Tsinia, the Changlins desire for it to be understood that the Tsinians possess a queen not only by title but as a ruler and guardian. It will bestow onto them hope through this dark period. Do you retain a Torpas with the gift of Mynd?"

"Certainly. I will attend to it. A message will be dispatched without delay."

"Be certain there are precautions," she said. "I desire that the message reach Celdor Cavern. Athania dispatched birds with reports of our arrival, yet I am certain they were intercepted, as we happened upon too many perils. Also, see that intelligence is spread to the Outlands. It would be valuable to happen upon aid during our travels."

"It will be done," he answered, and then departed, leaving Thya alone with her thoughts.

THE VULTENS

It was getting late and Thya yawned yet again. She needed to sleep and feel rested for the journey ahead, but her mind would not settle, even for one moment. Until it calmed, until she stopped feeling agitated, she would not be able to sleep. Plus, the Torpas had gone to so much trouble to show their love and support for her and their quest, it made it hard to leave. She feasted with them, joined in their song and even danced with Alkazar. She looked around at the faces of the Torpas. They were no longer strangers but kinsmen, as much as the citizens of Tsinia were.

"Queen Thya," Lance, one of the wisest of the Torpas called. She smiled at him. "Can I interest you in on of our delicious meat pastries? My wife was up all night baking them."

Thya patted her belly. "If I were to consume another morsel, I believe I would pop. Do not repeat this, but I have consumed three of your wife's pastries previously and they are wonderful. They are one of my preferences from the filled table."

He clapped his hands together. "Oh, Queen Thya. This news will astound my wife. I appreciate your remark and will pack the remainder with your provisions for the journey."

"You are too kind."

His face turned red and he bowed, then turned to relay the news to his wife. Thya giggled as she watched him skip and do a joyful jump.

The following day, Thya, Alkazar, and Somal set out on the remainder of their journey. They were dressed in new attire. A group of female Torpas had presented Thya with a silk cloak made from a material so light that it felt as though she wasn't wearing it, and yet the cloak possessed warmth like a fur coat. It was unique, and unlike anything she had seen in Enumac. Even now, she was still being surprised by the magic of the land. And now it was about to become her permanent home and dear sweet Alex – she wiped away a tear – Alex would stay in England and never learn of his ancestry. He would live a safe and happy life.

Alkazar and Somal were dressed in similar cloaks, but in darker colours. Somal lifted a satchel, which Thya assumed was food, and Alkazar held the canisters of juice and refreshments. Again, she was not permitted to carry anything, no matter how she argued.

Many of the Torpas stood outside the cave and called out farewells and good wishes. Thya returned their gestures with a wave and her thanks.

Omad remained with the Torpas, as Thya had requested, and did so without argument. She thought that might have something to do with Alkazar being with her.

They travelled through Death Valley. There were no more giant sand worms, although Thya remained alert and anxious. Alkazar lightened the mood with song and laughter. Somal had been quiet at first, but Alkazar made sure to involve him in the discussions by asking for his opinions. Thya wanted to walk beside her love and entwine her hand in his, but according to the code it wasn't allowed. Thya was royalty and was expected to lead, with those below her status following. She couldn't help but turn her head to try to catch Alkazar's eye. On the third try their eyes locked. He smiled, and the butterflies in her stomach fluttered. She wanted to stare at him all day and night, still not believing that he was alive. She looked ahead again and pursed her lips to stop from giggling like a school girl whose crush had just noticed her. Alkazar made a formidable soldier, she mused, and with his gift and increase of power, she felt sure they would succeed in locating the Darkeye.

It was midday when they left Death Valley and met the formidable icy mountains of Klon. It astounded her that Enumac could go from one extreme to another in just a few steps. *What a peculiar place.* She swallowed as the white, icy tips of Klon beckoned to her towards the foot of the mountain and wrapped her cloak closer as the cold bit into her skin.

"It will become warmer once we start climbing," Alkazar said. "May I?" he asked as he held his arm out.

Thya nodded, afraid that if she spoke her teeth would chatter. She stepped into his arms and his warmth defrosted her chill from the inside out. The trek up, around, or across, whatever route they had to take, didn't look too kindly. She sighed but was resolved in her decision.

"We will rest here for a while. We may have a difficult trek ahead of us."

Alkazar went to move away and she grabbed his arm. "Don't," she whispered.

They sat cuddled together, now they had an excuse to touch. Alkazar didn't waste any time. He moved his hands in gentle circles on her back then bought his hand to the nape of her neck, drawing lines across her skin. She shivered. "Alkazar?"

"Yes, my love."

"Do not begin something you cannot conclude."

Alkazar removed his hand from her neck and returned it to the outside of her arm. Thya huffed but heard him chuckle. He knew of her frustration and she knew of his. They both closed their eyes, knowing that when the time was right, they would make sensual but passionate love together.

Somal found a large boulder a short distance away and kicked up gravel and dust as he hastened towards it to relieve himself. Once he returned, Alkazar stood up and walked over to the same boulder. Thya laughed. It reminded her of lining up for the toilets at a bar or nightclub. Before her mind regressed further into the past, her stomach growled. So loud in fact, that Somal turned towards her and raised his eyebrows. He took out one of the carefully wrapped meat pies from his rucksack and handed it to her. It tasted heavenly. The pastry was flaky and the meat soft and juicy. She wondered what meat she was eating and studied the colour and texture of it. She didn't recall seeing a cow or pig anywhere in or near the caves of Torpas, although it wouldn't surprise her if they had their very own Grenko among them. But a Torpas who could make a cow or pig appear … She was drinking berry juice when that thought came to her and laughed at the same time as swallowing. The juice went down the wrong way and she had a coughing fit. Alkazar and Somal ran towards her. She held her hand up to stop them, trying to get her breath back.

"My Queen," Somal spoke with authority. "Permit me."

He stepped in front of her, raised her head, and ran two fingers across her neck. The choking stopped.

"You have quite a gift, Somal." Her throat didn't feel sore and when she spoke it didn't come out with a wheeze. She smiled and cleared her throat, even though she didn't need to.

"What occurred?" Alkazar asked.

"I attempted to consume and drink at the same duration. My throat was not vast enough."

Alkazar laughed and Somal joined in. It was a wonderful sound. The two men ate while she found a different rock to do her business in private. Once they were packed, they started to climb. It wasn't how Thya imagined people climbed mountains. They had no rope or safety harnesses, but they didn't need them. The path was almost flat and zigzagged across.

After several hours they reached the first peak. A green valley lay beneath them and Thya took a moment to take in the sight and breathe cool crisp air. She sighed before continuing down what looked like the safest route. There was still some light but, even so, the Tril moon would soon be upon them and she could not waste time admiring the beauty of the land.

The closer Thya came to the bottom, the more apprehension she felt. It was as though the mountain was telling her not to leave its safety. She pulled her cloak tightly around her and stepped onto the soft green grass of the valley.

Although the weather was kind and the way forward looked welcoming, she could not shake off the feeling of facing an unknown adversary.

"Alkazar, who inhabits these parts, for I sense we are not alone?"

"Tis believed that Vultens, a tribe of cannibals, exists here," he answered, and shrugged. "Though I have yet to sight them."

"Since you have not laid sight upon them, that does not suggest they do not exist," Thya said, surprised by how laid back he was about the situation.

"Inform us, Alkazar, of these creatures. What are we to expect should we happen upon them?" Somal asked.

"Firstly, my good friend, they would happen upon us. Vultens are cannibals as I previously stated. They are male in gender and breed amongst themselves."

"Are you remarking that the male Vultens reproduce?" Thya asked.

"Tis so, my queen. However, tis their provisions they are reproducing."

"They consume their young? How revolting," she exclaimed.

"Not all find this a tragic conclusion. Tis said one in five of the young is permitted to exist."

"Barbaric!" Somal said.

Thya turned to face him. "Though I will concur with you, tis the only path the Vultens are acquainted with. Tis their nature and they see not error." Even with that said, she had to wonder if it were wrong to feel repulsed by it. "The Tril moon will presently be upon us. We ought to locate a suitable place to respite until the following light."

Alkazar agreed. "The terrain ahead appears smooth enough for slumber."

"When we are settled, employ your gift of illusory and let it appear that we camp amongst thirty Boras. Tis prevention against attack. Still, we require a watch. The initial I will perform, as I am unable to slumber as yet."

"It will be completed, my queen."

Once they found a suitable site to camp, Thya walked towards a nearing forest to look for wood whilst Alkazar and Somal set up camp. Her thoughts returned to Alex. She wondered what he was doing at that moment and if he was missing her.

Thya stopped walking and turned her head from left to right, searching, listening. Goose pimples covered her arms. She discarded the wood and ran as fast as she could to the others. In the pit of her stomach, she knew that something was wrong. She had wandered too far from the camp and, by the time she neared it, strange voices stopped her. She crouched behind a bush. A group of primitive-looking cavemen surrounded Alkazar and Somal. The savages were naked, their bodies covered with course hair. The hair on their heads was long and matted. They were thin, ribs showing through their taut skin.

Although she could not understand what their grunts and screeches meant, fear mixed with anger as she watched them prod and push Somal and Alkazar around. They waved sharp arrow-tipped spears at them and tore at Somal's clothing. Others prodded Alkazar with their spears. Blood seeped from the cuts and the Vultens bent their heads and looked at one another before stabbing their skin again.

Thya wanted to rush out and stop them but she would be outnumbered and still was not sure of what she was capable of. So many ideas raced through her mind, but she rejected them all, and watched helplessly as the Vultens tied Somal and Alkazar to two wooden poles.

The Vultens grunted excitedly as their dinner struggled to get free. Once the Tsinians were bound and prodded enough, the grunting and screeching reduced to mumbles and the Vultens departed. She wasn't sure why.

Staying hidden, she concentrated on Somal's binds, willing them to undo. They did so without resistance, but he barely had enough time to run towards her voice before the Vultens returned.

They screamed and shouted at one another when they saw his pole was empty and started on Alkazar, seeming to blame him for Somal's escape, even though he was still bound to the wooden stake. Fortunately, they were too busy screaming at each other to search for Somal. But how was Thya supposed to help Alkazar without being captured herself?

The Vultens began pushing each other, and the

screeching rose to such a pitch that Somal and Thya covered their ears. The Vultens' arms flew around as they slapped and bit each other. Their blows became harder and their screeches turned into snarls. One of the Vultens lunged towards his opponent and stabbed him with a spear. He pulled the weapon out and watched the body fall to the ground before roaring triumphantly and pushing his way towards Alkazar. The other Vultens moved aside quickly but jumped with excitement as he walked up to Alkazar and plunged the spear deep into the left side of Alkazar's body, just below the ribs.

Thya froze as Alkazar's cry pierced her heart. She stumbled back as his blood soaked the ground. Fire burned through her veins. Pain fuelled her anger to the point where she no longer felt emotion. It wasn't a numbness as such, more of a crazed calmness, and it awoke a dormant memory from a time where she had experienced a similar reaction. Thya listened to the inner voice that told her to let go and a surge of energy crashed through her.

There was darkness, and peace, and nothing more.

***

Somal watched dumfounded as Thya stood up and walked towards the Vultens. He should have restrained her, but her movement was so quick and sure. He had no time to react and now it was too late. "Nay, return, my queen," he yelled.

She turned her head until her gaze was upon him. He stepped back and tripped over his own foot, landing on the dusty ground. The thing looking back at him was not his queen. The whitest of lights shone from her eyes. Her hair, now the purest of white, fanned around her as though a wind was blustering, and her lips were the colour of darkness. This was the dark arts, he concluded, and shuffled further away as his pulse raced.

Thya turned her sight back to the Vultens. They had stopped their ravings to gape at her. Somal remained hidden, unable to turn away. Fear rooted him.

The Vultens stared at her, transfixed by the light she emitted. She moved forward, her long gown skimming along the ground, yet Somal firmly believed she was gliding, rather than walking. When she halted, the Vultens grunted in a low continuous tone and then screeched, high. One dared to stepped towards her but then retreated while the others gestured for it to keep moving. Somal guessed they had never seen anything like this before, as he hadn't. He knew very little about the Tsinian queen. Only what Valcan had told him. Now he realized that his father had left out some important details. Unless his father did not know about the dark spirit that lived within their queen. But surely Alkazar retained knowledge. Or did she have everyone fooled?

He peered around Thya and saw Alkazar limp on the pole with his head slumped onto his chest. He had lost a lot of blood and needed Somal's aid but fear, or maybe cowardice, froze his feet to the ground. He watched transfixed as another Vulten dared to approach Thya. This one looked more cautious. The cannibal bent his head to the side before taking a step forward then squawking and jumping back before repeating the process.

Thya raised her arm and swung it carelessly to one side, as though shooing away a pesky fly. The Vulten rose from the ground and slammed against the sharp rocks of the mountain with a series of bone crushing snaps.

The effect was immediate. The Vultens ran at her, screaming and waving their weapons. But they never got anywhere close to her. She dispensed of them in the same manner, throwing them aside with her will. One of the creatures hurled a spear which was supposed to skew her, only she diverted as soon as it departed the Vulten's hand.

Somal saw Alkazar attempt to lift his head but then it fell back down. He thought it better for him not to be alert whilst Thya was possessed. Thya leaned towards the remaining Vultens and Somal heard what sounded like a snarl. The Vultens stepped back, looked at the Vulten beside them, and then as though their minds had been programmed, they turned back to Thya, silent and unmoving. It was as if they had been frozen, but there was no ice upon them. *So, what is keeping them in a mesmerized state?* It had to be Thya, he mused. *She retains the gift of Mynd?* The only Bora to possess Mynd was the Dark lord of Senx – Kovon. Somal shook his head as he tried to get around the fact that Kovon and Thya both possessed evil within them and yet had fought against each other. One wanted to destroy Tsinia and the other to save it. His head hurt just thinking about it. He blinked and continued watching his queen.

A white beam of light, which Somal assumed came from Thya's eyes, split into five white rays and landed on ten of the unfortunate Vultens. Screams pierced the air as flames exploded across their face. Their hair and skin burnt fiercely. The stench was sickening, and their agonizing screams difficult to bear.

Somal now witnessed Thya's true strength. An evil power that no Tsinian should possess. He never imagined such evil existed; it was neither defence nor justice.

Determination cancelled out his fear. He stood up and marched towards her. Alkazar, now alert, cried out a warning, but it was too late. Thya spun around. Somal barely caught a glimpse of her before he was lifted from the ground and catapulted backwards. The left side of his body slammed into the mountain. An agonizing pain swept through him as he slipped into darkness.

***

"Thya, nay!" Alkazar yelled, but it was too late. Somal's body was on the ground unmoving. Thya turned to finish her slaughter, only the remaining Vultens had fled.

Alkazar cleared his dry throat and spoke in an authoritative manner. "Thya, be attentive to my tone. You hold trust in this voice. If you heed, set your sight upon me."

She glared at him. Her eyes brightened and Alkazar recognized she was close to attacking. What act could he perform? He was bound to a stake and barely had the strength to lift his head. Nevertheless, he was determined to return Thya, even if it took his final breath.

"Thya, tis Alkazar, your love. Take heed."

The glow diminished slightly. She leaned her head to one side and stared at him as if mulling over whether he would harm her.

"Thya, pursue my voice. Tis calming to you. When you locate the voice you will locate me, Alkazar." He was not sure if he was getting through to her; still, he had to try. "Thya, return to me. I will remain."

It had worked once before, only he could not reach her. Whatever possessed her had a will far stronger than her own. Another wave of pain hit him, and he panted while waiting for the tightness in his chest to subside. Too much duration had passed, and he worried that he would bore the entity and she would destroy him in the same manner she had the Vultens.

"Thya, you are within a cave. There are tunnels left and right, do you sight them?"

He hoped this would succeed. Something about the way she appeared made him think of a Gestle – an underworld demon once spoken of in fables as warnings, and then forgotten.

"I sight them," a ghostly voice sang out.

Alkazar's heart lightened, and his pulse raced as sweat dripped down his face. He was certain he heard Thya's voice within the ghostly song of the Gestle, if that was what it was. But he had found her, and if she was to return to him, it was imperative she locate him.

"Thya, be attentive to my voice. Pursue the sound. I desire for you to enter the right tunnel. I am located on the completion of your path."

Her expression changed. The lines of concentration disappeared, and her creased brow smoothed. Her eyes dimmed, and as she stepped forward into the invisible tunnel, she collapsed to the ground.

Pain overwhelmed his relief, and this time he could not contain it. He choked on burning sour vomit and used the last of his energy to glance back at Somal, who was unmoving, and then to Thya. She, too, was unconscious and surrounded by the burning bodies of the Vultens. Alkazar felt spittle drip from his mouth and down his chin. Unable to hold his head up anymore, it slumped forward, and he hung from the pole like a lifeless puppet.

***

Thya heard a voice calling, but it grew fainter and, no matter how fast she ran, she couldn't find it. She turned a corner and an awful stench hit her. It went down the back of her throat and made her gag. She opened her eyes and found herself laying in the dry dirt. All around her lay the smouldering carcasses of what used to be Vultens. Somal lay in a heap some distance away. Her eyes then searched for Alkazar and, when she found him, she screamed his name.

The Vultens had killed him and Somal.

She couldn't turn her head and not see the crispy bodies of the cannibals. They were scattered everywhere. But what had happened to them? Why were they all dead?

She desperately wanted to get to Alkazar to see if he was alive but barely had the energy to lift herself into a sitting position. Only once had she felt so weak, tired, and helpless.

"Alkazar," she cried, but her voice came out as a whimper and was cut off by dry hacking. She coughed, her chest tightening as she fought for breath. "Alkazar." Even raising her voice drained her of energy.

Alkazar's head moved as he slowly came around.

"You are breathing. Praise the Changlins," Thya cried.

"Undo my binds," he whispered. "Concentrate. You are capable, Thya."

She screwed up her eyes and concentrated. As weak as she was, and using only her gifts, she could not undo the ties. She felt the last of her strength leave her body and sagged to the ground.

***

Alkazar felt his binds loosen enough to move his hands and wrists until he felt the rope slacken. Once he was free, he crawled to Thya and rested her head in his lap, caressing her face until she opened her eyes.

"Alkazar, I was not certain. I retained a belief that they had eliminated you. I am uncertain of Somal's state. Examine him, it could be that he too requires aid."

"Rest now, my queen. I will locate shelter and examine Somal." He covered her eyes "You are away from harm now."

Her eyes flickered shut and he shook his head. Even now she remained stubborn, trying to fight sleep. Pressing his fingertips to her temples, he massaged them until she was asleep.

***

Thya awoke in a cavern of some sort. The roof was so high she couldn't see the top. She shivered, and it wasn't from a chill. She was not alone.

"Show yourself," she called out. Her voice cracked so she repeated herself with more authority. "I demand you show yourself!"

There was an echoed snigger as she waited for whatever it was to appear.

"My Queen, you are protected."

The voice pulled her out of wherever her dream had taken her. It was long gone, but not forgotten. She shivered, and her breath came out ragged. A hand caressed her face and she smiled. She knew that touch. She knew those hands.

Her eyes opened and she looked around, searching for the monster that had invaded her dreams. She opened her mouth to say something, but Alkazar put a finger to her lips.

"Be silent, my love. You require respite if you are to regain your strength."

She ignored his soft words and looked around the shelter he had located. A cave with only one exit. It was dry, and the small fire he had built kept the shelter warm. The candles he had placed around the cave gave them just enough light to see, but it was an illusion. A shimmer rippled across the entrance of the cave. Alkazar had used his gift to create the image.

"Somal," she cried and attempted to rise. "Is he…?"

"Nay, Thya, Somal is resting. He requires healing, as do you. I beg of you to slumber. You are protected. On this, you retain my oath."

"I am fit," she argued. "A little weary perhaps, but nothing that cannot be fixed with nourishment." She bent her head to the side and raised her eyebrows, waiting for him to elaborate.

"You suffered a fever. It has broken now. Nevertheless, I am not a healer."

"For what duration?"

"Two Tril moons."

"Nay, tis too much. What of my kinsman? What news of Tsinia?"

"Fear not. All is quiet," he assured her, although he had no way of knowing what was occurring in Tsinia.

"Partake of this draft. On learning of your arrival at Celdor Cavern, Valcan dispatched more of his wondrous tonic and I bought it along, should the requirement for its use arise." He sighed. "If only the Torpas healers knew of these recipes Valcan concocts."

Thya did as he instructed. She took three gulps and refused more. The tonic worked swiftly, filling her body like warm heat and she soon felt stronger, her mind clearer.

"That is much better. Now to you, Alkazar. You are hurt?"

"Tis naught. A scratch. Naught to concern with."

"Nonsense. Remove your garment and permit me to examine your wound."

He reluctantly took off his tunic. Her fingers traced along his skin and rested on his chest. He trembled, and she sensed his vulnerability. His heart raced beneath her touch, and his breath quivered. Her own chest rose and fell erratically. They needed each other. She could not ignore the pull and brushed her lips against his before kissing him with so much passion that she felt as though she was melting. He held her neck and waist as he deepened the kiss. Thya moaned and he dominated her mouth with his tongue. But soon, too soon, they pulled away from each other to catch their breaths. He cradled her face and kissed her. She responded by pulling him closer and wrapping her arms around him. Their embrace became urgent and she wanted him to take her, but they were not alone. She satisfied herself by running her hand back over his skin and he winced.

"Oh, my love. I forgot you were hurt."

She cleaned the laceration with a damp cloth before ripping the bottom of her dress and wrapped it tightly around the wound. For all the blood he had lost, the wound wasn't nearly as deep as she had feared.

"Does it pain you much?"

"Nay, I had forgotten, until your caress. Tis naught but a scratch."

Thya tutted. "More than a scratch. My brave Alkazar, naught can ail you, can it?"

He touched her arm and she felt the pull of desire again. Thya shook her head and looked down to the ground. "It requires healing," she announced, fixing her gaze on his arm. He opened his mouth, but she quickly added, "You voiced previously of Somal requiring a healer. Are you familiar with one?"

He sighed deeply and tucked a strand of her hair behind her ear. She knew that was about as intimate as they were going to be.

"There is a sorcerer in the valley of Imas. When you regain your strength and Somal has woken we will journey there. I am certain he will bestow aid to us all."

"Once again you voice in riddles, Alkazar. Why would I require aid?"

"My apology, my Queen. The Torpas' unhurried dialogue has passed onto me."

A loud cough from the corner of the cave tore their attention away. Somal sat propped up against the wall of the cave. His arm was in a sling that Alkazar had created from one of the canvas bags. His grin was wide and infectious. "My queen, tis fine to sight you in good health. Alkazar, we will create a healer of you yet."

Alkazar helped Thya stand and they walked over to him.

"You are well? Not in pain I trust?" she asked.

"Very little," he replied. "Yet I yearn to partake in my father's side-line of natural medicine for I am certain there would be herbs in this region that would cure our ailments.

"Potion remains," Thya said.

Alkazar left to retrieve the flask. As with Thya, he had swallowed barely a mouthful before waving the draft away.

"Alkazar, permit me to care for your wound."

"Tis naught, Somal, do not be concerned."

"How did we escape?" Thya asked.

Somal's brows lifted. "Are you not aware? Do you not recall?"

Thya watched as Alkazar and Somal exchanged a quick glance.

"What is being held from me, Alkazar? I demand to be informed of what occurred. Enlighten me on why the Vultens lay burnt at my feet."

Alkazar sighed. "What do you recall, my queen?"

She shut her eyes. "I recall sighting a Vulten assault you with a spear and felt intense anger, but I remember nothing else. I awoke to discover the Vultens dead and Somal and yourself unresponsive."

"Have you experienced this intense anger previously?" he asked. He took her hand and raised it to his lips to softly kiss it. "Continue, my love."

"Certainly, I have experienced this rage previously. A warmth courses through my body and the intense fury causes me to black out. On one such occasion I woke to find myself in the forest of Tsinia. Soon after that, the body of Siren was found, and you were arrested for her murder."

Thya's hands shot up to her mouth and she muffled a scream. Being unsteady on her feet, Alkazar helped her to the ground.

He then turned to Somal and looked at him gravely. "What you will discern cannot depart from this cave. You will bestow your declaration."

"I swear by the name of the Changlins that I will not repeat what I am to perceive."

Alkazar nodded. "Tis acceptable. You have both our existences in your hands."

Somal nodded.

Alkazar then turned and faced her. "There is an additional will, a spirit of sorts, deep within your soul. I believe the spirit surfaces when you feel threatened. You are unable to obtain command of this energy and are not answerable for the damage it causes. Twice now I have witnessed it, and twice I have drawn you back. Nevertheless, the most recent was not effortless. Tis as though the force has increased its power over you, that by some means it is increasing in strength and I fear it is attempting to obtain entire control of your body and soul. You do not recollect the possession and possess not a command of the second will. I will not accept that the energy is totally evil, otherwise, I would not be present. I have discovered much, though I dare not probe further for fear of causing lasting damage. The sorcerer I voice of possesses considerable powers and is capable to rid, or at least aid you, in mastering this force."

Somal remained silent.

Thya however, had many enquiries. "So, it was I who eliminated Siren?"

Alkazar took her hands in his. "Nay, my queen, it was the second will that removed Siren's existence. You are not responsible. I realized the council would not comprehend and—"

"You accepted the blame," Somal interrupted, "understanding that your breath would be removed?"

Alkazar nodded. "Thya is exceptional, more than you deem. If she had forfeited her existence, it would have affected us all. Consider for a moment, where would we be presently. Everything has a reason for being; each individual has a vocation, and Thya, you have yet to uncover yours. It was not your turn to pass over, nor was it mine, it seems." Alkazar smiled.

"And the Vultens?" she asked.

He described what he had seen when he was conscious. When he came to the attack on Somal, she gasped in horror and wept.

"I would never have intervened," Somal explained.

"Only I sighted an entity was not my queen. You did not possess command and I do not lay responsibility on you. Both can be confident that your secret will never leave this shelter."

"Why though?" she asked. "Where does this power, this evil - and I will name it as such - where does it originate?"

Alkazar shook his head. "I have not awareness of why and when. Nevertheless, I deem it concerns your association to the Changlins. Your power still astounds me. I believe I have yet to witness your full potential and, until you can command the force, I refuse to probe further. Thya, I am anxious for you. I had a trying task returning you. I am concerned that on a following possession your soul will be captured forever."

"Then we ought not to irritate our queen," Somal joked.

Alkazar smiled, grateful for his lightness.

Thya looked into Somal's eyes. "In England, we possess a word – Sorry – to imply regret and apologize for an effect we completed or voiced. So now I declare to you, Somal, how sorry I am for my act upon you."

Somal shook his head. "There is not a requirement for your regret, my queen. You are not the cause of my hurts. This force, the will, was not of your own. There is naught to absolve. Though, if you will permit me, I desire to converse openly."

"Continue," she said.

"I had not the opportunity to encounter you before. I had only perceived your talents from the elders, my father voices highly of you. Your powers and strengths are legendary to Tsinia. However, absolve me for this."

Thya nodded for him to continue. "I sighted you as a beautiful princess who unbelievably defeated the warlord and who is the saviour of our land. Yet you appeared helpless and understandably scared. Nevertheless, I have sighted - in the duration I have been in your company - your gifts, and you retain strength and a determination that I have yet to sight in another. I finally appreciate why you were selected for this quest. You were born a Ganty and thus far have owned the title. I am honoured and fortunate to be in your service."

Alkazar knelt beside them and Thya placed one arm on his shoulder and the other around Somal.

"Oh, how fortunate I am to be enclosed by such love and loyalty. Together, my friends, we will succeed."

FATE AND KARMA

Thya didn't want to waste any more time, so they continued their journey at the crack of light. The valley of Imas lay between the mountains of Klon. Although the trek wasn't particularly hard, Somal was struggling. Thya did her best to walk at his pace. It hurt to see his strained face, and the panting and sweat mocked her. He was having a hard time and it was her fault. When Alkazar had asked him how he as doing, he was in so much pain he couldn't even speak. He grimaced what she supposed was meant to be a smile and waved his hand as though brushing the comment aside. He continued without complaint, but he needed aid quickly, and Thya needed some answers from the sorcerer.

Light was starting to fade so they made camp. Somal was finally getting some of the rest he needed but Thya was unable to sleep. She knew – no, she had always known, that she had killed Siren and her unborn child. Until now, she refused to accept or admit the truth. Alkazar had done a great job of tricking her into believing he had taken their lives, but only she could have burnt the Vultens alive. Where had this evil spirit that Alkazar spoken of come from? How was she supposed to control it, before she lost herself completely?

Each time she questioned herself, and blamed herself for the murders, she sank deeper into despair.

A Tril moon passed before they reached the border of Imas valley. Enir lived in the mountains of Klon, and Thya could see yellow lights flickering in the distance. It was high up, and she wasn't looking forward to the climb. She was tired mentally and physically and, if time wasn't pressing, she would have suggested making camp again.

There was just enough light left to see. No one spoke. She guessed the others were as exhausted as she was. Alkazar walked behind her. She turned her head now and again to look at him and was greeted with a smile or a wink. She had called him over earlier and asked why he wasn't walking beside her, only to learn that it wasn't allowed. No one could walk in front of her, which was a ridiculous rule, and she was quick to remind him that they were no longer in Tsinia

A Bora dressed in red trousers and a floor length jacket waited at the bottom of the jet-black mountain, ready to great them. "Enir the majestic awaits you," he announced. "Accompany me."

Thya nodded her acceptance and was the first to follow.

"Sorcerer Enir expects us, how so?" Alkazar asked.

"Enir the majestic perceives all."

"So, your master is familiar with our plight?" Thya

asked.

"My master perceives all."

She wondered how long the servant had been waiting. Did the sorcerer use a crystal ball, or something similar? How did his power work?

They eventually reached the home of the sorcerer, only it wasn't the kind of home Thya was used to seeing. His house was built into the mountain itself. Only the face of the house could be seen from the mountain steps. They all stared open-mouthed as the servant escorted them through each roomy cavern. Thya wanted to walk slowly and take in the warm and inviting décor, but the servant hurried them through.

He stopped walking and ushered them into one of the largest rooms. It was bursting with refreshments and a blazing fire crackled, warming up the cold stone of the mountain. The sight of the food lightened Thya's heart while the heat thawed her tired limbs.

"The healer is to accompany me," a servant said. His sudden arrival made her jump. "You are requested to consume and respite. There are fresh garments in the adjacent room."

"Relate to your master there is not requirement for this indulgence," Thya said.

"My master anticipated your remark and bade me to reply. 'You are a monarch and special guests and will be treated as such.' Will the healer acknowledge himself, for my master awaits?"

"I am he that you require," Somal answered and then left with the servant.

Alkazar and Thya didn't waste any time in tucking into the delicious feast. She hadn't realized how hungry she was. Soon after, with her stomach full, she felt sleepy. Relaxing on Alkazar's chest, she closed her eyes. However, her thoughts were filled with images of home and of Alex.

"My queen, you are silent and deep in contemplation," Alkazar said. "I fear your qualms are numerous, unburden them if you will."

"'Tis the uncertainty of what will transpire. The fear for your well-being and that of my kinsmen and not knowing the outcome. Will I ever sight my residence again?"

"Your dwelling is presently in Tsinia," Alkazar reminded her.

She knew that, but it was England she was thinking about, yet she wasn't ready to reveal her secret. Oh, how she wished Alex was here, so they could embrace their son together.

Alkazar cupped her chin and turned her face to his. "Your fears are many and only duration will tell. The only reassurance I can bestow is to remind you that, though your travels carry uncertainty, and danger will pursue your every footfall, the rewards you will obtain are new awakenings and understanding."

Thya nodded. From the first moment she had stepped on Tsinian soil, her eyes had been opened to new experiences and understandings. Even with what had passed and with the predicament she now faced, she regretted nothing. The more she thought about it, the more fortunate she felt. Even with the terror she had met, she wouldn't give any of her experiences back.

For the first time since her arrival she felt relaxed, and soon fell asleep, nestled in Alkazar's arms.

It seemed she had barely shut her eyes when she heard her name being called.

"Enir the majestic does not communicate orally, he will converse through mind," the servant told them.

There was a basin of steaming water and a pile of towels sitting on a cabinet. Someone must have put them there while they were sleeping. Thya and Alkazar washed and took a moment to hold one another. It seemed a long time since she was this close to him. She lifted her head and kissed his lips. It was all the reassurance she needed. As they sat and waited, they couldn't take their eyes off each other. She didn't know what he was thinking, but she could have drowned in his eyes. Her palms sweated in nervous anticipation. Before long, the sorcerer entered. A tall thin man who carried an air of power stood in front of the them. Thya stared into his yellow eyes then slowly carried down and looked at the flowing green embroidered gown he wore. Before she could examine him more, a voice echoed through her mind.

Your companion is resting and will recover presently.

Alkazar nodded.

Could he hear Enir too?

Tis well you presented him for his strength was fading.

She gasped and Alkazar's eyes widened, neither of them had realized that Somal's injuries were so serious. He could have died, and it would have been her fault. She should never have insisted they travel all this way. She should have found aid for him sooner. She didn't know how, but she pledged to atone for her crime against him.

I understand why you are present, Queen Thya, only tis not prudent to eliminate the force which you possess, not at this instant.

I – how – can you hear me? she replied with her mind.

Alkazar's eyes were fixed, but then he nodded. Emir had not spoken. Was he having two conversations at the same time? How could he do that?

Thya worried she might think something private and Enir would hear or see it.

The sorcerer smiled. *Queen Thya, please, concentrate on your breathing. It may help if you close your eyes.*

Breathing? He was speaking to her in her own dialect. How was that possible? She turned her thoughts off, now that she knew he could hear what she was thinking.

She took a deep breath and tried again. I understand what you're saying. But if this is what I want, can you remove the second will?

Yes, he replied. *However, I am not in favour of this.*

Alkazar frowned and she shook her head. She didn't want any secrets between them. Enir, I wish to hear what you are saying to Alkazar, unless I shouldn't.

Very well, he answered. You retain modest faith in your queen. She is more powerful than you envision. She is your queen and saviour, which you fail to recall. Though Thya is your lover and confident, she is firstly your queen. Your place is as her subject and you will continue so until the duration arrives when she forms a title for you. Your position is a pace behind and, yet you lead. You ought to abide by Queen Thya's command and yet you command her.

Thya smiled despite herself. She didn't think

Alkazar had ever been scolded like that. But when he looked to the floor and shuffled his feet, she felt his embarrassment. Alkazar sighed before raising his head again.

The sorcerer continued, You have achieved much to have arrived at this distance and it will be your love for one another that will maintain. Do not renounce hope, Queen Thya, for your resolve approaches. Rest a while then tis necessary for you to persist with your journey. In three Tril moons, Celdor Cavern, will be besieged by Kovon's army.

"Then I will depart at once!" she cried out.

Your companion is not yet fit to travel, and this crusade will not be successful without him. You are right to worry. However, listen to me. The Tsinians will defend themselves and, unless you fail in your quest, everyone will be victorious.

How is it you know all this? she asked.

I see everything.

Do I find the Darkeye? Do I defeat Kovon?

Emir shook his head and smirked. If you learn the outcome before you act, then you have no future. You control your own destiny.

Enir turned and left without another word. Thya stared at his retreating back. "Prudent man," Thya said, with a draw of sarcasm.

"He is ancient, Thya, and gifted beyond words. I retain no knowledge of what was conversed between you both and I do not desire to learn of this, only take heed in what he remarked. Tis an honour. I desire to converse more."

"And I suppose he will hold the knowledge to all?"

she replied mockingly.

"You are offended?" Alkazar asked.

"Enir sights all, yet he will not reveal the outcome to me."

"Could it be that he is not permitted to disclose the outcome? He remarked to me that tis your power and courage that will serve you. You will succeed, this is assured."

"Then I hold naught to fear."

"Nay, Thya, do not assume this. Tis why Enir would not disclose your outcome. There is a great deal to fear and retain in mind that destiny is not predetermined."

"As usual you are just. Pardon me, for I am anxious to conclude this and return to my kinsmen."

"I realize this. Rest now upon me and I will ease your troubled mind."

Thya lay on his chest while he gently massaged her temples. Warmth emitted from his fingertips and he soon soothed away all her worries.

After a calming sleep, they washed, dressed, and got ready for their departure. The room was again laden with food and drink and, as they started to eat, Somal arrived.

"How do you fair?" Thya asked.

"I have not rested so soundly since our departure from Celdor cavern. And you, my queen, all is satisfactory?"

"I have not located the response I was seeking; however, my mind is clearer, and I feel positive that we will be triumphant," she lied.

No sooner had they finished eating, Enir appeared. *I bid you all a fond farewell and desire that good fortune follows you along your continued journey.*

He handed Thya a small kernel. *I speak only to you now, Thya. Listen very carefully. Take this seed, so named the seed of hope. Only when hope fades should you eat it. You have only one use, so think carefully before you do. Remember, only when there is no more hope. This is very important, Queen Thya.*

He bowed respectfully and, with a swish of the tail of his quilted coat, he left.

Thya put the seed into a pocket sewn under her skirt.

Guides escorted them from Enir's home and down the steps of the mountain until they reached the border of Imas valley.

They thanked their guide and then continued.

Alkazar was unusually silent. Thya thought Enir might have said something else and it was bothering him. He walked with his head down.

"Alkazar, why so silent? What ails you?" she asked. She didn't like seeing him so down.

"My pardon, Queen Thya. I am in awe of Enir and remain puzzled. I desire to encounter him again and spend much duration. A strange aura surrounds him. Just being in his vicinity leaves me tranquil."

"I agree, Alkazar, and yet he did not answer any of my queries."

They looked at one another and laughed.

Although they both worried about the future, they continued the journey in high spirits. They talked of Tsinia, at least what Thya remembered of her land. She spoke of England and Somal had many questions. They talked for so long that she wasn't surprised to see the sky darkening.

"The Tril moon will soon be upon us, we will rest here. What remains of our journey?" she asked Alkazar, as they sat on the ground under the shelter of a large tree.

"We have covered much of the route. However, the valley within the mountains of Klon has been kind to us. The terrain, now, will become difficult. See ahead." He pointed to the north. "We need to reach the peak and then make our final descent. Once on flat terrain we should discern the city of Helkon."

"Then we should respite. Allow me to take the initial watch," Somal said.

Thya shook her head and pulled her knees towards her chest. "I am not able to slumber, at present. Rest you both. I wish you an undisturbed sleep. I feel we have a difficult journey ahead."

Somal turned away and lay down with his back to them. Soon, he was snoring quietly.

Alkazar smiled at Thya and she smiled back.

"Queen Thya, are you resolved to proceed to Helkon?"

"With certainty," she replied. "Why such an inquiry? If you are informed of my fate then be silent, for I do not desire to be acquainted with it. What will be will be. Do not permit what Enir whispered to trouble your heart. I cannot comprehend what will occur in Helkon, or how I am to obtain the Darkeye. However, I do not intend to fail and if by probability I am not to depart from Helkon, I can assure you, my love, that I will not be taken silently."

Alkazar smiled warmly, but Thya knew her words carried no weight.

CITY OF HELKON

The tall white walls surrounding the city of Helkon came into view as they started their descent down the mountain. Thya's heart beat at twice its normal speed.

"Tis prudent I employ my gift of Dispelling in cause of an attack," Alkazar suggested.

"Excellent notion, the element of surprise. Somal and I will walk ahead."

A large metal fence stood on the top of white sand walls and the magnificent wooden gates slowly opened as they approached. Two unarmed guards stood in wait. Another two Boras similarly dressed in black and gold armour stood further across from one another, further inside the city. Their sight fixed straight ahead, as they spoke in a tongue Thya couldn't understand. The guards bowed down respectfully to her and gave Somal a quick glance as they stepped into the city

"Tis unproblematic. I expected some difficulty,"

Thya whispered.

"Too effortless," Alkazar's voice agreed. "Perhaps tis why I sense a feeling of dread."

"Why such pessimism?" Thya smiled. "Maybe tis possible to gain the Darkeye without combat. Do you not concur?"

What was she saying? She knew the quest wasn't going to be effortless. Thya swallowed as she heard the wooden gates close with a growl as though there was a dragon or some other monster guarding the city. Thya swung around and looked behind her, just in case. The two guards that had bowed to her now stood behind her. The other two walked slowly in front. Somal had paled, and she wondered if he had come to the same conclusion as her, that they were trapped.

Thya raised her head and attempted to keep up. Flat farmland lay to the left of them and in front, the city floor was covered with stalls of all sorts. An arrangement of strange characters sold spices, materials, animals, and even slaves. The variety of these various coloured inhabitants, some with more than one eye, others with no nose, surprised her. She had never seen anything like it. Thya was disappointed with the fast pace set by the guards. She would have loved to explore the city. Unfortunately, she was here on an official visit, and followed the guards down the narrow path that led to the palace.

A stone castle, shaped like a sandcastle, stood before them. Two stone pillars marked the entrance of King Theon's stronghold. Alongside the palace lay a valley of round clay houses, each dwelling surrounded by a small plot of farmland. She couldn't see a single resident but assumed they were in the marketplace purchasing their daily stores.

Surprisingly, she felt optimistic and without fear as she stepped over the threshold and into Theon's domain. It felt strangely familiar and comfortable, as though it wasn't her first time in the city.

They had reached Helkon, a feat that had seemed almost impossible not so long ago. And with the gracious introduction and acceptance into the city, she believed their quest was coming to an end. She hoped her fellow Tsinians felt the same. But looking over to Somal, she saw him shake and gulp. his eyes widened as he took in the sight of the castle's entrance. Once they entered the palace and the large iron doors closed behind them, Somal leaned in. "I do not believe tis prudent to proceed any further, my queen."

The quiver in his voice made her curious. "Why so?" she whispered, taking smaller steps to prevent the guards from over hearing.

"Sight the palace guards, my queen. They are a race named Rants – part Bora, part vermin."

It was then Thya realized that the four guards that had escorted them through the city had been replaced by six formidable looking guards. It wasn't just their ghastly over-sized rat heads, or their large front incisors that made them look vicious, it was everything. Their size, their full silver metal armour, the almost sneering mouths as they stared back at her, as if they knew something she didn't.

"Tis observable," she said with a shaky breath "I sighted numerous species within the city. What is your concern, Somal?"

"Rants attacked Tsinia under Kovon's command. We had not sighted the race formerly, and presently I comprehend why."

Thya felt the air leave the passageway, squeezing her lungs. Every fibre in her body quivered with the sudden change and it had nothing to do with Somal's statement. Their footsteps and breathing seemed to increase in volume as though they were walking through a tunnel, not a roomy passageway. She glanced again at a Rant and, although it looked hostile, with its sinister sneer, it had no weapons. Even so, something was off and, every step she took, the brightness slipped further away.

Alkazar's invisible hand squeezed her own. Did he feel the change as well, or could he sense her fear, she wondered? Thya nodded her head slightly and squeezed back. She straightened her head and shoulders, before turning to Somal.

"Display not fear. I will protect you. This is my word."

Somal straightened and Thya took a deep breath before walking towards two huge cream-coloured doors adorned with gold leaf décor. They opened wide as they approached and displayed a decorative throne room. The ornate gold leaf designs and paint gave the room a regal feel. But her sight was on the large Bora who sat upon a throne of gold. He was dignified and important-looking but not fierce and powerful like she imagined he would be. His green tunic matched the back cushion of the throne. A rich red cloak hung around his shoulders. He wore a dagger, which looked like it was made of frosted glass, on his belt. His jewelled golden crown sat upon his head and the red ruby sitting in the middle was hard to miss. The king motioned them forward. She never took her eyes off him. Theon's face was expressionless. She couldn't tell if he was happy or angered to see them.

He gestured for an attendant to approach. The servant, dressed in a black long robe, stepped before Thya. Keeping his head bent low, he held out a small silver bowl.

She peered inside, recognizing the glittering gold substance. As was the custom, she dipped two fingers into the bowl, pulled out a pinch, and dabbed it over her lips. Somal followed suit.

"Salutations," Theon said. As expected, they both understood. His voice was loud and dominating, his smile false.

"Somal, step frontward," Theon ordered.

Somal did as he was told and took a calm and prominent step towards the king.

"You are the son of Valcan and belong to the generation of Languil. You possess the gift of healing and, although youthful in era, you retain extensive intellect. Swift in knowledge, courageous and loyal."

Somal didn't look surprised by Theon's knowledge. Thya sensed that there was a lot more to King Theon.

"Alkazar, son of Kapil, step frontward."

So much for the element of surprise.

It seemed pointless to ignore the king's command and as Alkazar stepped forward his cloak of invisibility disappeared.

Theon grinned with smug satisfaction. "You are a tutor of the arts and recently retrieved the employment of your gift." Theon tilted his head as though waiting for an acknowledgement, but Alkazar didn't oblige. The king continued. "I also retain awareness of your flight from Tsinia. You are a noble Bora, Alkazar, and your valour is one that I have not happened upon yet."

Alkazar remained silent and stone-faced.

"Step frontward, Thya, Queen of Tsinia. Although I retain acquaintance of your individual talent and can sense your fortitude and bravery, there is an obstruction that I cannot break. You maintain your deepest thoughts and nature buried. This formulates an inquiry. What are you concealing? You are obstinate, Thya, yet demonstrate a courage that cannot be matched. Tis remarkable that you reached this juncture, for I dispatched countless obstacles to prevent, or at least hinder your progress."

She stiffened as his words sunk in.

"Yet, here you stand." The king stared at each of them in turn before stepping down from the throne. "Why are you unique?" he asked Thya. "You set a puzzle. It will be satisfying to discover the secret you bear. I will require all that I desire."

He stood in front of Thya and they faced each other silently. His jet-black eyes widened as he took in Thya's shapely body. When he reached out to touch her hair, she recoiled, her face turning into a grimace. Alkazar struggled behind her, seemingly unable to step forward. He twisted his body, trying to pull out of whatever spell was upon him. His lips were pursed in concentration. Somal too was routed to the spot and, unlike Alkazar, after struggling for a moment, he gave up and stayed still.

Theon laughed.

Thya stepped up to Theon. "Release them," she warned.

"Do not attempt to employ your gifts, Tsinians, for they will not perform. You are already acquainted with this, are you not, Alkazar?"

Alkazar scowled at the King, avoiding Thya's eye.

"He was warned by the sorcerer that you would lose your power if you entered the city. All of you are powerless." Theon's gaze returned to Thya. "I am acquainted with why you entered the city. Unfortunate that the Darkeye was destroyed in Senx, is it not?"

Thya tried to move towards the king, but her feet were also glued to the floor and she struggled for a few seconds before giving up and scowling at Theon.

He smiled again. "What I marvel at is how you proposed to complete the task. Were you going to request it?" He laughed.

Somal clenched his jaw. "Why does your army assault our city when we have not acted against you? Tsinians are a peaceful nation. You have not cause to harm us."

"Be silent!" Theon ordered.

Somal fell to his knees with a mumbled scream, his hands searched frantically for his mouth, which had disappeared as if his face never had an opening.

Thya couldn't move, but she still struggled to get her hands on him. She wanted to rip Theon apart.

"You do not retain the privilege to address me. Do you not comprehend where you stand? Do you not fear me?" The throne room darkened as Theon's power grew, draining it of light. His stance changed going from small and regal looking to that of a terrifyingly evil enchanter. If she was able, she would have stepped back in fear.

"I am King Theon," he bellowed, "I am the greatest of all. Sorcerers quake in fear of me. Down on your knees."

Although she tried to resist the force that was pulling her down. she was overpowered, as was Alkazar. They joined Somal on the floor. The darkness faded and light reappeared; the room was as it once was.

Breathless from struggling, Thya panted as she raised her head and glared at him. "Enough of this. What is it you desire?"

"I desire naught. Are you surprised, Thya? Nay, I do not require the power of the Changlins. Tis Kovon's desire, not mine. I have not requirement for additional power. Yet I am acquainted with where they dwell. Do not be discouraged, Queen. You failed in your quest and will encounter your doom in Helkon city, but you ought to be content with your strength and the distance you journeyed. You accomplished where numerous would have failed."

Thya, used her strength to pull herself up. With no movement, a chanted spell, or even a blink from Theon, the spell was removed and Thya stood up straight, her fists clenched by her side.

"I have not failed yet!"

Theon laughed. "Tis what Kovon expressed. I understand why you satisfy him. Thya, the name evokes a vision of beauty and yet tis your will and determination that draws Boras to you. I am indecisive about what to do with you; we will converse once you have been educated in befitting conduct. Remove them," he ordered.

"What of my companions?" Thya shouted.

"They will forfeit their breath for their defiance and decompose within the dungeons. My guards relish in torture. I am certain they will be eager to encounter our new guests."

"If you harm them, I will personally tear you from limb to limb."

Theon did not laugh, and he did not reply. He removed the gag from Somal as four Rants appeared at the door. Theon, without words, nodded to the Tsinians, and Somal and Alkazar were pushed out of the room.

"Do not surrender hope," Alkazar shouted as a Rant grabbed his arms and started to drag him away. Two Rants stood beside Thya, one of their clawed hands grabbed her arm, but she pushed it off.

"Do not touch me," she warned. and walked out of the throne room. Theon's laugh echoed at her back.

Before the Rants pulled Alkazar and Somal into an opposite tunnel to the one she was directed towards, Thya called out. "Be strong, my Tsinians." If only she would listen to her own advice. The human side of her nature was shaking inside. If she didn't have control of it, she knew she would have collapsed on the floor in a panic attack. But Thya was a Gantie, the strongest, most powerful of all Tsinian's, and she was far from giving up, even if her powers had been stripped from her.

***

Alkazar kept his eyes on Somal as they were led through a maze of narrow tunnels and down several sets of stairs into the bowels of the castle. Somal stared at the damp, smelly walls and arches, looking anywhere but at the Rants in front of them. Shackles dangled from the guard's waist, clinking with every step. Somal had yet to be incarcerated, and Alkazar understood what fear and thoughts might await him.

Alkazar's fear was for the fate awaiting his love. If there was any possibility of escape, how would he locate her? While he had breath left in this body he would not renounce hope.

The guards shoved Somal and Alkazar into a cell. The cold stone blocks dripped from damp and it smelled of rot and death. Somal had paled, and his eyes were wide in fear. When the Rants came back in, Alkazar straightened his back but, as quickly as the urge to fight came to his mind, it left. It would be a dumb, maybe even deadly move.

Two of the guards grabbed Somal's wrists and chained them to shackles. "Alkazar," he cried. His voice was barely a whisper to begin with and was drowned out as the Rants pulled his arms over his head and locked the shackles to the metal rings overhead.

"Be courageous," Alkazar said. "We will prevail. Appeal for might."

Alkazar's arms were shackled too, and he was hauled up until his arms were stretched. His feet barely touched the ground. Behind him, somebody else entered the cell. The Rants grunted and sniggered as the backs of their shirts were ripped open.

Somal cried, though he did not sob. His chains

rattled as his body shivered. There was nothing Alkazar could do for him. "Be courageous, Somal, maintain your sight upon me and do not turn aside, no matter what will pass."

The first stroke hit their backs simultaneously. The leather whip ripped into their skin. Searing hot pain sliced through Alkazar's back. The whole of his upper body shook. Beside him, Somal gritted his teeth and squeezed his eyes shut as his body spasmed.

"Nay, Somal," Alkazar cried. "Maintain your sight upon me!"

The second blow was dealt to Alkazar as punishment for calling out. There was more force behind this lash and he gritted his teeth, refusing to cry out. He kept his eyes on Somal as the strikes came out of sequence. Every lash located a piece of untouched flesh. Somal's body shook but he kept his eyes open. Alkazar continued to offer him support and, on every occasion, was dealt a harder blow as punishment.

"Seal your mind," he called out in a strangled cry. "Visualize a pleasurable moment."

For a moment there was a reprieve, but then his hair was yanked and twisted so his face was turned away from Somal. The largest Rant leaned close to Alkazar and screamed at him. Spittle flew in his face, and he returned the greeting with a smile before laughing. Laughter turned into a chortle and then a coughing fit, before Alkazar laughed once again. The Rant screamed again before releasing his hair. Alkazar continued coughing.

Both lashes struck Alkazar's back. He had no energy to turn and look at Somal, but he was satisfied that his punishment, at least, had stopped. Alkazar refused to cry out or concede defeat.

Time passed, and he lost all feeling. He heard the whoosh of each strike but felt no pain. He took his strength from knowing that Somal was not being punished, and took his consciousness to another place, leaving his broken body chained in the cell.

*****

Thya stared at the cold, damp-smelling stone wall of her cell. It felt strange to be without her powers, and yet there was something there, although caged, that told her she wasn't completely powerless. She had no idea where Alkazar and Somal were, only that they had been taken in the opposite direction.

The cell had few furnishings. In the far corner was a wooden bed, beside which stood a decrepit table with a pitcher and a large clay bowl. She had only a moment time to glance around before the Rants shackled her to the wall.

Mumbles and excited chatter echoed from behind her. She knew from the way she was chained up that she was going to be whipped, but she wasn't frightened – she was angry. What right did King Theon have to punish her? Or to hurt and separate her from Somal and Alkazar? Who did Theon think he was? She couldn't wait to see him again and imagined getting her powers back and ripping him to pieces. Thya shook her head, wondering where that violent thought had come from.

She didn't fear death, far from it. After all they had

been through, how close they had come to completing their quest, to have it ripped from her grasp at the last hurdle left her angry, not scared. Thya felt as though everything was coming to an end. But she wasn't going to feel sorry for herself. She did, however, mourn for the loss of her son. She would never see him again and she hadn't even had a chance to say goodbye. Would his life turn out the same as her own? A lie; being adopted and never knowing his true birthright. The injustice of it made her fists clench. Now the end was near she hoped her demise would be quick and without pain. but the sound of a whip hitting the concrete floor behind her, made her close her eyes and breathe shakily. No, death she didn't fear, but pain she did. Trying to forget about her impending torture, her thoughts turned to Alkazar and Somal's fate. She prayed to the Changlins that their suffering and death would not be prolonged, and that Theon's description was merely a threat. She doubted it, it was obvious Theon intended to keep to his word.

How close was she to the Darkeye? How would she have located the crystal? Was she going to ask for it? Whatever, it was hopeless now. Thya bent her head low and her shoulders dropped. It was hopeless … She remembered the seed of hope that Emir had given her. If there was a time for it, it was now. Only she could not reach it. Even the seed of hope was hopeless. She sniggered at that thought.

There was further laughter, murmurs, and then whispers in a language she couldn't understand, followed by silence. She felt a rush of cold air as the back of her dress was torn open and a wet, leathery touch slide from the nape of her neck to the bottom of her back. She didn't know if it was a finger or a tongue, but her body recoiled. The Rant standing behind her laughed, though it sounded like a wheezy cough. Maybe that was the way all the Rants laughed. He grabbed a fistful of her hair and pushed it to one side. His laughter turned into a strangled cry and something thudded to the floor.

She didn't know what had happened, but the effect was immediate. Someone unshackled her and led her over to the bed, then gently pushed her down to sit. The guards rushed out and the iron door slammed shut behind them.

Thya sat stunned, shaking her head as she tried to understand what had just happened. She ran over to the door and leaned her ear against the cold metal, hoping to hear something, anything that would give her some answers. But there was only silence behind the door. Thya paced the room, rubbing her neck and her aching wrists. She thought through everything that had happened since being pushed into the cell. None of it added up. One thing she was sure of, though – they were frightened of her.

Thya took the seed of hope out of the pouch and stared at it as she questioned whether it was the right time to eat it. Only she realized that, although she had almost given up hope, she was unhurt and alive.

She returned the seed to the pouch and lay down on the bed with a yawn, curling into a tight ball. She was exhausted, but sleep wouldn't come, not while she was worrying about Alkazar and Somal. They were in danger. Hurt, possibly tortured, but she felt in her heart that they were alive. How was she supposed to help them? It was her job to protect her kinsmen but, without powers and not knowing where they were being held, her escape and their rescue seemed unlikely. Thya turned, hoping to get more comfortable on the hard-wooden planks that covered the stone bed.

The door to the cell unlocked and Thya stood up. King Theon slowly entered. Almost cautiously. With his hands on his hips, he tilted his head and his eyebrows creased. The king pointed to her and then to a bowl that his servant held out. Thya peered into it and saw the same glittery substance that she had used in the throne room. It seemed stupid to refuse him. She did as she was told and, once the spell touched her lips, Theon's words became clear.

"Rotate," he commanded.

She turned around as instructed. A Rant pushed her hair aside, exposing her bare back and neck.

"'Tis so then," Theon exclaimed.

Thya turned around to face him. "What is so?"

He bent his head to the side, and his eyes widened. "You are not aware?" He stepped back. "Yet you possess the ancient emblem."

"What ancient emblem? Will you not reveal the significance?" She would not beg even though she needed answers.

Theon's sudden change of behaviour concerned her. His stance and facial expressions went from awe to surprise, then almost to fear. His head tilted again, and his hand rested on his chin as he walked around her.

"Do you not comprehend your greatness? Do you

not realize who you are?"

"Of course, I am Queen Thya of Tsinia, Guardian of the Changlins."

"Have you not marvelled at the difference with yourself and that of other Ganties? Surely you have experienced strength and a will that cannot be bested?"

"With certainty."

"You possess the emblem."

"What emblem?"

"Upon your back."

"'Tis naught but a birthmark."

"Nay, Queen. You are mistaken. The mark as you name it, is an emblem of exceptional greatness. I understand now why your thoughts were blocked from me. Immortality appears with a value. I wonder what you would bestow for the quest of eternal youth?"

Nothing he said made sense to her but, before she could demand answers, the King jumped up and down and rubbed his hands like an excited young boy. "I will present you to the Bustak, as homage," he said, rubbing his hands together as a huge smile etched on his face.

His next words were foreign to her. The magic of the spell had worn off, so she just stood and watched the Rant and the king communicate, hoping to get an idea of what was going to happen next.

Theon grinned and patted the guard's back. They spoke briefly and nodded their heads as they continued to stare at her. She wished she understood. Who or what was the Bustak? The name raised goose pimples on her arms, and the belief that this was, again, the end of the road for her returned.

The guard led her from the cell and back into the

palace. There were no shackles, no Rant gripping her arms. They walked beside her but kept glancing at her. She ignored them and concentrated on calling out with her mind. *Alkazar, my love, where are you?* She repeated it over and over, with no knowledge of whether he could hear her but, if he had, there was no answer.

Six Rants escorted her to two large grey doors and motioned for her to enter, but they would not go any further. She walked into a large room full of giant steaming baths. The fragrance of forest berries filled her lungs. The doors closed behind her and she walked forward. Five female pygmies dressed in togas greeted her. The tiny slaves guided her towards the nearest bath and removed her ripped dress before motioning for her to enter.

The last thing Thya expected was a bath but, as the opportunity was there, she stepped into the warm, soothing water. She hadn't realized how dirty, bruised, and battered her body was. It seemed so long since she had last washed, and she was keen to rid herself of the grime and trauma. She looked over her shoulder, half-expecting the Bustak to appear, whoever that was, but when no one came she closed her eyes and tried to relax.

Her failure to complete the quests and protect her friends weighed heavily on her mind. Tears rolled down her face and she allowed them. One of the pygmies gently massaged her temple. She didn't care if she was showing weakness. She was a woman and had emotions and she was tired of having to be strong, and so she cried and sobbed.

The bath was warm, yet it wasn't water that she

bathed in. It was the same liquid they had in Tsinia – thick, almost creamy, yet transparent. The strange water and the delightful fragrance incited visions of Tsinia, which had become all but a distant memory until now.

She thought of her beautiful, peaceful city. The quaint tree dwellings that her kinsmen lived in. The little wooden bridges and the glorious lakes she used to bathe in. She swam in the happiest of moments in Tsinia – and the memory of lovemaking with Alkazar. A memory of Alex followed, and the dread of never seeing her son again. He would never learn about his father or his inheritance. She had failed to retrieve the Darkeye and it was unlikely Tsinia would ever be as it once was. She was sure Kovon would poison and destroy everything good about Tsinia. Her kinsmen, although safe for now, would eventually be found and turned into slaves. And what would become of the Torpas? What of the Changlins? She had failed everyone.

As if the pygmies could read her mind, they soothed her with song.

She wanted to stay in the bath. She didn't want to face what came next. However, she was eventually ushered out. Her hair was dried and combed until it shone. Her nails were manicured, and her face made radiant by special ointments. Though she allowed herself to be pampered, she couldn't help feeling that she was being prepared as a sacrifice.

Whilst dressing, she retrieved the seed of hope from her discarded skirt and hid it in the silk slippers she was given to wear.

She was dressed in a flowing white gown with long, bat-shaped sleeves, and a gold braided belt. At the very moment the pygmies stopped their pampering, the palace guards opened the doors. Just seeing a Rant made her skin crawl. She had felt safe with the Pygmies. They had been kind and gracious to her. Now reality returned.

Thya turned and smiled gratefully at the Pygmies. The gesture was returned but with it came with a look of pity. She understood then that whatever the Bustak was, it was not to be thought of lightly. Although her situation was grim, it was not knowing what was going to happen that gave her just enough hope to hang on.

THE BUSTAK

Two Rants held Thya's arms in a tight grip. They escorted her out of the castle and into a small building adjacent. There was hay on the floor and barrels stacked. It looked like some sort of wine cellar, but this was Enumac and she doubted it was the kind of wine she knew in the bottles laying on the wooden racks. Dust fell as one of the Rants pulled a chain from the middle of the floor and a door opened out, revealing a set of grimy steps that led into the dimly-lit underground. Flickers of light told Thya there were flamed torches at the bottom of the steps and thankfully not darkness. After reaching the bottom of the steps, a sandy tunnel barely wide enough to fit through lay before her.

The worm tunnels twisted and turned and, although she tried to memorize the way, it wasn't long before she confused the lefts with the rights. The Rants however, knew exactly where they were going, and didn't pause once. they took her further and deeper and she wondered how far underground they had travelled and how the hell she was going to find her way out.

Eventually, they came to another set of stairs, these were made from stone and began a further descent. After a while, the stairs turned sharply to the right. Thya stopped walking and her mouth open as she gasped.

They were in a huge cavern with torch lit walls that seemed endless, and a ground that couldn't be seen. Thya wondered if they would ever reach their destination, for it felt as though they had been walking for hours.

The stone steps were slippery with water and she had a difficult time preventing herself from slipping. There were no walls on either side of the stairs and no banisters.

Twice she had to grab hold of a Rant to keep her balance. She continued following them until they stopped so suddenly she bumped into the leading guard.

Thya gasped again at the sight before her. It looked as though she was in the middle of nowhere, stranded on stairs suspended by nothing. The Rants pushed her down onto the next step, seemingly refusing to go any further themselves. The leading guard motioned for her to continue.

Taking a tentative step, she turned to see the Rants walking back up the stairs. Thya sat down on the cold wet step and put her head in her hands. How the hell had she got into this mess? And what was she supposed to do now? Was she supposed to wait here until the Rants returned, or starve to death? The only other choice she had was to continue her descent, but she had no idea what waited below. Too tired and anxious to think about it, she decided that for the time being, she would stay where she was, and rested her head on her arms.

Time had no relevance, not that she cared how long she sat there. Eventually though, she got up and continued downwards. The torches continued to give off a yellow light but the ones in front seemed to dim with every downward step she took. The darkness crept closer the further down she went, until only one step was left alight.

Thya stopped walking. This final step might be her last. There was something waiting for her, something vile and evil. The rot of decaying flesh assaulted her nostrils and went down her throat, making her gag. She could turn and run, but to where and to what future?

Putting her right foot forward, she stepped into darkness.

Her foot landed on solid ground and, at that exact moment, torches around the chamber flared with light. Her eyes closed from the sudden brightness and slowly she opened them again. Her eyes adjusted, and she listened for any movement, knowing that she was not alone. Apart from dripping water there were no sounds, and no one to be seen.

"I sense your presence, Bustak, come forth."

No sooner had she spoken, a vision appeared. A huge, floating mass of jellied flesh bobbed in front of her. There was no head, or body, and its only facial feature was a blinking eye in its centre. A red beam emitted from its ruby-red iris, landing on her chest.

Was this the Bustak? The creature she'd feared?

"Appearances can be deceiving, Queen Thya." No

mouth opened, yet the Bustak's voice was stern and demanding. "It was inevitable this encounter would occur, and I have remained for some duration to sight you. Do you know why you are in my presence?"

"I have been detained against my will, as I am sure you are aware. I have been enlightened to the fact that I am to be a sacrifice to you."

"A sacrifice?" His laugh quivered, as did the jellied flesh. "Nay, Thya, tis not the concept. King Theon realized your true potential and dispatched you to me and he will be greatly rewarded."

"If not a sacrifice, what do you desire from me?"

The Bustak remained silent for some while before speaking again. "Do you not sense the spirit?"

Her stomach dropped. "What spirit?"

"Have you not questioned where your strength and power originate from? You are unique, Thya, and yet unaware. I will not harm you. However. you will remain among your fellow Gestle for eternity."

To learn that she wasn't about to die should have meant something to her, but the Bustak's statement unnerved her. Who or what were the Gestles and how could she live forever? She wasn't immortal. "If I possess this spirit, a strength and power unlike another, why do you presume you can detain me?"

The Bustak's laugh echoed through the chamber. "I deem tis the duration for you to discover who you are. Permit me to introduce you to your kindred."

From every dark corner of the cavern, female Boras dressed in long white gowns identical to hers, appeared. Their hair fanned around them as if an invisible wind blew. They glided forward, their feet hardly touching the ground. Their arms stretched out and long fingernails curled from their pale soft hands. It was their eyes that frightened Thya the most. It wasn't because of the bright white light where their pupils should have been, it was the feeling of deja-vu, but more than that. Their appearance felt familiar.

The Gestles' light shone into her eyes, but she did not turn away. Their gazes locked on hers until the Gestles, as if silently commanded, looked away. Their attention was directed to the Bustak, their master.

"I am not familiar with these Boras," Thya said.

"Nay, you will not be. They are ancestors of Boras and yet a unique species. They are named Gestles and were formerly powerful sorcerers who ruled the Outlands. Presently, they are demons of the underground. A race driven beneath – persecuted for their strength."

"Are they evil?"

"What is evil, Thya? Who boasts the authority to judge what is error and what is just?"

"To slay unnecessarily is error," she answered.

"If tis so, then are you not evil?"

He could read her mind. She forced her thoughts to clear.

"Nay, Thya, tis not your thoughts I examine, tis your heart. You retain sorrow for your act and believe you ought to be punished for removing Siren's breath. I judge that you will never absolve yourself and the act will haunt you ever more. Why though? You acted on your natural, basic instinct and retained belief that she merited fatality. Why do you not accept this? Why does it pain you so? Permit the spirit to engulf you, permit it free rein on your soul and you will experience guilt no more."

Thya looked again at the white demons. "Nay. The act I committed was in error. I believe this deep in my heart. I was not myself and had not command of my actions."

"Tis accurate, Thya. Lay vision upon them. Do you not sight a resemblance?"

She took in their matt black lips, white irises, and silver hair. Shaking her head, she turned back to the Bustak. "Are you remarking that the spirit I possess is that of a Gestle?"

"With certainty." The Bustak laughed.

"Tis not feasible," she argued. "I am of Tsinian descent. My parents were the rulers of Tsinia. I am the rightful queen."

"Tis also actual, alas Tsinia no longer possesses a queen and presently it will cease to exist. Kovon's army marches to the caves of Celeron and will presently enslave your kinsmen. Concern yourself not – your fate is written."

"Then I have failed," she whispered, and bowed her head. "I did not locate the Darkeye and my kinsmen will suffer in cause of my defeat." She felt sick. She wanted to cry. She had failed everyone.

The Bustak laughed again.

Thya's head whipped up. "Mock me not!"

It continued to laugh. The echoes bouncing off the stone walls. When it stopped laughing, it glided towards her. "Though you were a ruler, for a short duration, you are not shrewd. Have you not yet comprehended that the Darkeye exists not?"

"Nay!" she cried. "I was dispatched by the Changlins to retrieve the Darkeye's twin."

"Thya, I will not mock you, yet state how naive you are. I presumed you understood and that all would develop apparent."

Thya put her hands on her hips and scowled at it. "Now that you retain me under your command, why do you not clarify what is meant?"

"Tis righteous. Tis why you are in attendance. Previous to Boras and Senx, Gestles and warlocks governed the Outlands. They existed in harmony, pending another race happening upon them, and branding the Gestles evil. Some fought against the violence and were permitted to exist serenely among the new race.

"Enumac existed in colonies till greed took hold. Boras divided, creating the Tsinians and Senx. The Senx would not permit the Gestles to govern them and so presided over their own land, creating the premier warlord. Gestles formed the code of honour and ethics and ruled Tsinia, which grew and prospered. Ultimately, the Gestles disregarded their unique powers and, as you ought to have deduced, were recognized as Ganties."

She shook her head. Ganties were the ancestors of Gestles? Underworld demons? But what made her so special?

Before she could finish analysing and, as if reading her mind, the Bustak continued. "The Gestles who favoured a fight were banished and received refuge here, in the catacombs of Helkon. You are home, Thya. They are my servants. Yet you radiate superior power and so will present you as their ruler. Tis a great honour

I bestow upon you."

Thya needed time to think. "The Changlins were controlled by the Gestles," she said, though it was more of a question.

"Yet it was not control," it said. "Following the unification of Gestles and Boras, Gestles created the Changlins, passing their spirit into them."

Thya gasped. "Then Alkazar was just in his remark. Tis *I* that commands the Changlins?"

It laughed. "You are establishing comprehension."

"I am. Tis the spirit of the Gestle that instructed me to proceed to Helkon and created a false quest – not to discover the Darkeye, but to discover who I am."

"With certainty and, now that you comprehend, you can permit the spirit to occupy and develop into what you are destined to be."

"And if I permit this spirit, what occurs to Thya?"

"Thya will cease to exist. There is not another option. You cannot command the spirit, tis stronger than your own will, as you have discovered. The spirit has always existed as an element of your soul and you must accept this."

"If I accept it and again develop into a Gestle, then I have truly failed my kinsmen. I will never again sight my land and my love." *Or Alex.*

Its tone became harsh. "Even now you have failed. You cannot retreat. You are in my control and reside in my domain for eternity. As for your love, he barely possesses breath."

Thya felt a familiar burning course through her body - the change – and knew that if she didn't control it this time, she never would.

"The spirit awakens, Thya," the Bustak exclaimed, its tone lowering. "Permit it to flow over you. Do not resist."

Her body shuddered as she felt the spirit flowing through her like a powerful force. It took hold of every part of her body, apart from her mind. That entrance was blocked, and the spirit didn't force its way in. Thya was ready to surrender to it. There was no inner fight. *Could it be because of the Gestles' presence, or because I have finally learnt of my legacy? Or was it because I know that Alkazar is dying and that our son is waiting for us?* Whatever the reason, for the first time, she sensed the Gestles' power and yet had complete awareness of her own will.

She pushed her command onto the Gestles as the Bustak desperately gave orders for them to obey him. At the same time, Thya projected her thoughts to them. *No outsider had the right to, nor should ever control you.* They turned their tilted heads from one master to another. Thya sensed their confusion but needed them to listen to her commands. She gave them all her concentration, sight, and thoughts, and it was imperative that they listen to her and not the Bustack's commands. Again, there was no inner struggle, inside her mind. Thya looked to each one individually, enough time for them to understand her intentions. *I am your kin. A Bora born in Tsinia's borders, daughter to Ganties. I am the queen of Tsinia, guardian of the Changlins and your mistress. You will no longer take heed or follow orders from the Bustak. It has not power nor authority over you.*

"I am your Master. Take heed," the Bustak shouted, sounding more desperate with every echoed scream, Thya thought and then she smirked as his screeched out demands grew fainter, until her mind was once again silent.

At the same time that she turned her head towards him, thirty Gestles demons turned simultaneously; their sight now focused upon the Bustak, which was moving from side to side, but unable to mind connect, or escape from their powerful dazzling glare

Thya raised her arms. Mysterious wind blew around the cavern. She had only one command for the Gestles and that was to destroy. When she slowly raised her arms, the white from her eyes – from all their eyes – intensified.

The Bustak quivered, its red beam fading and, no matter how hard it tried to move, it was unable to float away. Slime dripped from its flesh as though it was melting. A gurgling scream came from the creature.

Thya absorbed its fear, her power growing with every second of its deterioration. The smell and sight were vile, so she closed off her senses. She needed to give the spirit full control of the mind and body if she was to destroy the creature. Thya took her mind past the Owto, a place where she wouldn't feel guilt or sorrow for what was about to happen.

The trickle of slime stopped, but the torture was far from over. She watched its putrid flesh pulsate and glow. A deep heat coursed through its jellied mass and beyond, turning into bright orange cracks surrounded by black, burnt flesh. The Bustak screeched as the blob distorted, each throb causing its shape to alter. The pulsating deepened and quickened, the mass started to swell. It ballooned, flesh stretching and thinning, until it finally exploded. Chunks of flesh splattered the ground until all that remained of the Bustak was a pool of slime, mucus, and membranes.

It was strange. Thya could see what was happening but had no interest in turning away or fighting with her internal will. The instant the Bustak was destroyed she regained her senses, but they hit her all at once. The putrid stench was too much, and she vomited. This time, the memory of what had happened remained with her. The Gestles stood silently, waiting for her command.

"I will depart, and I advise you, do not hinder my departure. I accept that I retain the spirit and that you are my ancestors. Exist in peace and there could be duration where you will again be permitted to exist as you once did. I will visit upon you to sight your progress. Only, it will be some duration until this occurs. Remember your past and what you formerly were. If you will it, it can be so again."

The Gestles bowed their heads.

Thya felt obligated to keep watch over them. Acceptance would take time, as would the thought of outliving the Tsinians, including Alkazar. But would she grow old? Would she stay the same age as she was now? No answers came, and she was too tired to think about the revelations.

Her strength had been sapped, her power depleted. She was exhausted, and her legs shook. But no matter how fatigued she was, the thought of Alkazar dying drove her on. Revenge pushed her onwards, and without realizing it, she had left the cavern and was travelling through the tunnels, her sense of direction on point. She knew exactly how to get out and where she was heading.

Eventually, she stopped walking. Her legs wouldn't take her any further, no matter how much she needed them. Her thoughts were blurry, and she felt confused as she looked around the sandy tunnels. They seemed to close in on her and she shook her head, taking deep breaths. The cloud of fuzziness disappeared, and she continued walking as if something pushed her onwards.

Before she realized it, she was standing outside King Theon's chamber.

An invisible wind blew open the great doors. The king stood up from his throne. "How? How can this be?"

Rant guards appeared on either side of her. She forced her will onto them, turning them to stone. They could neither move or speak yet were aware of everything. She wanted them to be witnesses.

King Theon stepped down from his throne and, in a fury, ran towards her. He cast a spell, but what it was supposed to do she would never know. The spell rebounded as though an invisible shield protected her. Theon summoned every ounce of his power and directed it at Thya. Sparks shot from his fingertips, but the shield continued to protect her. The spell rebounded and hit Theon, causing him to fall back onto the floor.

Thya strode towards him. A familiar burning in her blood began, taking her mind and will to another place as she allowed the Gestles' spirit to take over.

When Thya's will returned and she gained full control, she gasped, covering her mouth as she stepped back in shock. The gorgeous cream décor of the throne room was painted in blood. King Theon had been torn limb from limb, as Thya had first warned. His body parts had been neatly piled on top of one another. She knew this was her doing but there was no time to feel remorse. She turned around and walked past the stone guards, without thought or reason.

***

Thya had been given much to think about and yet, between fear and intense anger, she was able to control and focus on one objective: find Somal and Alkazar. She knew in her heart that they were both alive, but she couldn't sense them. Remembering the Bustak's words gave her more reason to hurry.

"Alkazar, perceive me. Tis Thya. I draw near. Remain with me, my love."

Sheer determination urged her on. Again, cause without reason raced through her mind. She pushed them aside. She wanted her thoughts to remain solely on Somal and Alkazar. The memory of her first meeting with the young healer and of the wonderfully unexpected reunion with Alkazar flashed through her mind. She smiled. They had found each other again, and there was no way she was going to lose him a second time. Nothing was going to stand in their way.

***

Somal's eyes snapped open the moment he sensed his power return. He sat against the slimy stone-cold wall of the cell. Alkazar's head lay on his lap. He stirred but didn't have the strength to waken. Somal began the process of healing him without delay, using all his skills. For a long time, he stared at Alkazar's face, waiting for him to stir. Alkazar opened his eyes at the same time the iron door to the cell swung open. No breeze was powerful enough to break an iron lock and there was no one waiting on the other side. Somal felt a shiver of fear before attending to Alkazar and helping him rest up against the stone wall. Alkazar sighed and then looked out at their freedom before he turned to Somal and smiled lazily.

Somal breathed deeply, laughed, and then winced as pain sliced through him like a searing blaze.

Alkazar sat up. "Somal, my friend. How do you fair? Are you capable to stand?"

"I am hurt," he answered, and took the arm Alkazar offered to push himself up. "It matters not. I will depart from this hell if it acquires my last breath."

"I will aid you and let us pray to the Changlins it does not come to that," he replied, and caught Somal when he swayed unsteadily. "Are you capable of travel?"

"If we are unhurried."

"Regrettably, we are in requirement of haste. The Rants will revisit us soon to continue our torture. When they discover we have absconded, our escape will be hindered. How I desire to encounter the chief Rant, for my hands itch to tighten around his throat."

Aiding Somal to walk, Alkazar checked that the passageway was clear before they left the cell. They walked through many corridors without detection but neither of them knew where they were going, or how close they were to freedom.

"Forgive me for asking," Somal said quietly. "Did you open the cell door?"

Alkazar smiled. "Nay, it was Thya." He stopped walking and held Somal back with his arm. "Be silent, I hear her call now."

"You do?" Somal looked up and turned his head, but neither saw or heard Thya. "Is she requiring aid? Where is she located?" he asked, eager to sight the queen for himself.

"Someone approaches," Alkazar warned, and used his gift to vanish.

Somal hid around the corner. He had no weapon, nor was he a warrior and, after being beaten with the Rant's whip, he would barely be able to swing a punch, but he would defend himself and Alkazar to the greatest of his ability. Grunts and moans echoed towards them. He could not wait further. He stepped out, ready to battle. Only the three Rants lay on the ground without movement.

"Come," Alkazar called out.

Alkazar gripped Somal's arm and pulled him away. He stepped over the bodies, stumbling to walk beside Alkazar though he was unable to sight his location.

The pressure around his arm vanished as Alkazar released his hold on him.

"I am certain if I focus, I can link with our queen and provide our location," said Alkazar from a few feet behind him.

"I desire that you appear to me when you converse. You cannot realize how unnerving it is to hear but not sight you."

Alkazar laughed. The echo rang through the empty

corridor, spooking him further, but he smiled nonetheless.

As they turned another corner, he fell to his knees and bent his head.

Alkazar reappeared; he, too, dropped to his knees.

"Arise, my friends," Thya said. "Your laughter carries, Alkazar, although tis fine to perceive." She laughed and ran towards them, gesturing for them to rise. Thya tried to embrace them both but Somal stepped back with a hiss.

"We must get you healed. Tis good to sight you both. I never renounced hope that we would locate each other again."

She took Alkazar's arm and led the way.

"How did you evade and where is King Theon? Are you marred?" Somal asked as he tried to keep up with them.

Thya stopped walking and turned, smiling at him. "Many inquiries. You are a curious Tsinian, Somal. Upon my gifts returning, it was not difficult to flee, and King Theon is on a break." She laughed, but Somal did not understand why. "I have not been harmed, Somal, I am merely tired. Respite will cure my ills."

Alkazar took Thya's arm, holding her up.

They departed from the tunnels and re-entered the castle. Somal was having difficulty travelling yet would not speak about the pain that racked his body, or the blinding headache that made him squint. No, they were all with breath, and freedom looked ever closer. He wanted to ask Alkazar if he was as surprised as Somal was himself by the absence of guards.

When they reached the main exit from the castle,

they were confronted by two Rant guards who barred their way with crossed spears. Thya stiffened, almost statue-like. The Rants didn't just lower their weapons, they stepped aside, and offered no further hindrance.

Alkazar gasped. "You retain the gift of Tracking, how is this possible?"

Thya smiled. "When Theon was destroyed, and our gifts were returned, more were bestowed upon me."

They stepped past the Rants and followed Thya out of the castle through the city.

This time the villagers stopped and stared. Somal was certain they were staring at Thya and at her clothing. Was he imagining it, or did they look frightened? Alkazar was too busy staring at the Rants to notice the villagers' reactions. The Rant army surrounded the market and yet not one attacked.

They quickly made their way through the city and out of the gates. Once alone, Alkazar stepped in front of Thya. "What transpired with the king?" he asked.

"I destroyed him," she replied sharply. "However, prior to his demise, I acquired further information pertaining to Kovon's escape from Senx. Omad had already informed me that a servant named Pacer aided in his flight. They travelled the Outlands in search of aid. Kovon was without vision, hearing, and dialogue, as were the afflictions I put upon him."

Alkazar's eyebrows rose and he stepped back. Somal had yet to perceive this information and, by Alkazar's reaction, he doubted Thya had spoken of the occurrence.

Thya continued walking, as though oblivious to Alkazar's reaction. "They arrived in Helkon," she continued. "The king pitied Kovon. He restored him and treated him akin to a son. Theon educated Kovon in the black arts, which aided him and increased his strength and malice. Kovon and his army of Rants were to attack Tsinia. However, when he sighted that the city was vacant, he was irate and burned down a lot of the forest, our kinsmen's abodes, destroying the Plecky and Recas, and seizing our lands. Now, I will take back what is rightfully mine."

"And how do you propose to accomplish this?" Alkazar asked.

"I will proceed to Senx unaccompanied, and I will eliminate Kovon."

Somal gasped and Alkazar stopped walking.

"Where is the Darkeye located?" he asked.

Thya stopped walking. There was a slight pause before she answered. "It was lost. It matters not. Tis not required."

"How are we to defeat Kovon without it?" Somal asked. "The Changlins voiced that only with the Darkeye could we be victorious."

"The Changlins were in error, Somal. The Darkeye is not required."

Somal shook his head. "Nay, at what duration have the Changlins been in error?"

Thya turned to address him, and her stare was cold. Somal swore she could have iced his body if she so chose. "Tis I that will defeat Kovon. Tis my duty and destiny, which I will fulfil, and I do **not** require the Darkeye to do so," she snapped.

"You lack faith in your queen?" Alkazar questioned

"Nay – nay," he stuttered and shook his head. "If

my queen states she will be victorious, then I retain belief in this. My enquiry was declaring that the Changlins have never misguided."

They continued their journey in silence.

HOMECOMING

Their first stop was the valley of Imas. Thya wanted to speak with the sorcerer again. She did not discuss her reasons with Alkazar, yet he knew. He sensed the change in her. An acceptance, somehow. What he did not know is *what* she had accepted, or the reason for her sudden alteration. She was quiet on the journey back but turned to him every so often and smile. He saw through the façade. There was no sparkle in her eyes and they did not crinkle as they once did. No, the smile was false. Thya was not happy. Alkazar wanted to talk with her, only he knew she would either lie or dance around the question. He needed to give Enir the chance to bring happiness back into her soul.

He glanced at Somal, who walked at a slow pace beside him. He was broken, not just from the beating, but in spirit. Alkazar hoped Enir would be capable of fixing Somal as well. As for Alkazar, the last time he had talked to the sorcerer, he had warned him to stop treating Thya as his equal, when she was clearly much more.

Whatever occurred in Helkon, it had forced her to distance herself from him. Maybe she had discovered he was but a lowly servant and no longer mattered to her. If so, why had she discarded him so easily? What use was he to her? Huh, even the Torpas had no employment for me.

He sighed and bowed his head.

"Alkazar," Thya called. He looked up and was surprised to see her standing beside him, her head tilted. "My love. What ails you? You appear so lost.".

"May I converse openly with you?"

"Certainly, we can delay our journey for a moment."

Alkazar paused, opened his mouth to speak, and then bit his lip before saying, "It matters not, let us continue. My thoughts can wait."

"Now I worry. Somal," she called. "Walk ahead. We will follow."

"My queen?" Somal questioned, as he looked to Thya and then to Alkazar, puzzled.

"There are no law or codes between us. Please, walk ahead."

Somal looked hesitant but stepped around Thya and Alkazar and walked in front, turning his head once more before continuing.

"You have enquiries, Alkazar, and I will answer them as best as I know, and if I am capable to."

He knew he wouldn't get all the answers he wanted but, in the hope of learning more, he took her hand into and bought it to his lips. "Thya, I understand our future has altered, that somewhere along the way, you have gained an understanding and lost a resolve. Where does that leave us? Where do I fit into your future?"

Thya squeezed his hand and smiled. "Naught has changed. My love for you has not diminished. Why would you believe that?"

"May I be candid?"

Thya nodded and raised her eyebrows. Her hands clasped tightly in front of her.

"I feel there will always be secrets between us and for this reason we can never be one."

Thya frowned and stepped back. "You are correct in your assumption that I have certain memories in my past, and even my future, that need to be hidden. You would not benefit from knowing. There are also secrets that I will announce to you when the duration is set. I promise. Does this not satisfy you, my love?"

"I am grateful for your understanding that there is more that will need to be conversed on this matter, but it can be delayed. Am I permitted to seal the promise with a kiss?"

He glanced around to make sure no one was watching, not that anyone was close by, apart from Somal, then grabbed Thya's waist and pulled her to him. His eyes took in her face and settled on her soft pink lips.

"Dear, beautiful, Alkazar. Kiss me, you fool."

***

Alkazar was not surprised to see Enir's servant, Narry, waiting outside the cave on their arrival. Thya followed after him, with Somal and Alkazar trailing behind. Narry stopped inside the same cave they had been in before, where the comfortable cushions lay in wait and another spread tempted them.

"Queen Thya and Somal are to accompany me," the servant said, gesturing to them.

Alkazar also followed and ignored Narry's instance that he remained and ate.

Enir stood outside a cavern chamber and waited. His arms were folded and his face a scorn. "Thya, Somal, please enter and I will be with you forthwith."

Thya bowed and looked over her shoulder and saw Alkazar attempt to follow, but Enir blocked the entrance.

"Alkazar I understand your want to remain with Thya, Nevertheless, you know from your own Tsinian healer Valcan that we require silence and solitude to heal. I cannot employ my ability if you are present with your insistence and worries. And the duration spent in your pleasant company causes your queen to suffer further."

'I understand very well, Enir, so should you, why I worry and require to be beside her and aid in her recovery. I implore you to permit me to visit her once you have employed your gift."

"Tsk tsk, Alkazar. You will be permitted to attend to your queen until she is completely recovered. Do not trouble my servants, they know their orders and will not permit you to pass. Be still and satisfied that Thya will get the best care and be treated as her title demands. Now I have laid on a feast for you, it would be rude not to consume and then rest."

Alkazar frowned but, out of respect for the sorcerer he bowed and did as he was requested and tucked into yet another wonderful spread of fruit, bread, and pies. Alkazar could only imagine what Somal Enir and Thya were talking about.

***

The other two entered a bed chamber and stood waiting patiently for Enir. When he appeared, he told Somal to leave with his servant. The two then bowed their heads respectively before leaving Thya and Enir alone.

Thya was unsteady on her feet and although he knew she needed answers, he deemed it best that she rested and was recovered first, both mentally and physically. She silently argued her case. *"You know what happened on Helkon. You know what the Bustak told me? Is it the truth? Am I immortal?"*

Enir remained silent, keeping his face placid as she continued arguing verbally, instead.

"I need closure. Don't you realize this? I need answers, Enir."

"You need to rest and recuperate. We will talk further once you regain your strength back."

Enir sensed her strength failing the longer she stood on her feet, but Thya was the most head strong Bora he had come across. It was when he saw her stumble to the bed, her legs no longer able to hold her weight, that he knew he would have to intervene. She shook her head and still insisted on answers. Enir did not want her to become unconscious. He wanted her sleep to be a natural one, but her stubbornness demanded that he act. He reached up and touched her forehead with his middle finger and caught her body, before gently placing her head on the silk pillow. He smiled down at her, before closing his eyes and placing both of his hands just above her head to begin the process of healing.

***

Somal's back was healed quickly, and he was told to join Alkazar for refreshments. The two friends ate and drank until their stomachs were full. They laid on the large silk pillows scattered around the rugged floor, and spoke openly about life in Tsinia and, in Alkazar's case, the Torpas. Neither of them mentioned what they had gone through in Helkon. It was something they would not forget, but it would be kept a secret. Their secret.

Enir appeared out of nowhere and Alkazar jumped as his voice rang loudly through his mind.

Somal forgot verbal conversation was not required and answered Enir's question out loud. "Do we possess duration to linger?"

Enir's voice echoed in Alkazar's and Somal's minds. *"Kovon has discovered that Thya is returning. He believes she has succeeded in locating the Darkeye and has ceased the planned attack on Celdor Cavern. Tis not Tsinians he desires. You retain duration to recuperate."*

Alkazar pursed his lips before thinking. *"Did not King Theon inform Kovon there was not another Darkeye? Was he not in cohorts with the King?"*

"Tis incorrect." Enir turned to him *"Theon took pity on Kovon, cured him from his aliments and gave him Rant guards to take back his land. Even so, he knew the evil in the warlord's heart and had not desire to involve himself further."*

Alkazar shook his head. "*I do not comprehend why Thya was informed of another Darkeye when none existed.*"

"*Ah, Alkazar. None will learn the reasoning behind this. Let it remain as Thya finding her path of destiny. I understand you require explanations. Alas, tis unlikely Thya will ever disclose the occurrence in Helkon. I sense your concern, only her fate tis written. You will cease your safeguard of her, for she is presently more capable than you could ever imagine. Have you not observed the alteration?*"

"*With certainty,*" he replied soberly. "*She retains gifts other than Yepsy and Flite. She has shut me out. I am not familiar with how to aid her.*"

Enir laid his hand on Alkazar's shoulder. "Events will never be alike. You are devoted to Thya and you will accept this, son of Kapil."

***

Somal and Alkazar spent two Tril moons resting and healing. Enir continued to refuse his request to visit Thya. Just when his patience was running out, he was allowed inside the chamber.

The first thing he did when he saw her, was to hold her tightly close to his body and squeeze.

"Alkazar – cannot breathe." Thya choked out.

"Oh, forgive me, my love." Alkazar released her, his face flushed as he smiled. "You are well?"

"I am. And Somal, how does he fair?"

"He is back to his talkative self."

Thya laughed. Somal was anything but talkative. "And you, my love, are you well?"

"With certainty. Somal's gifts almost rival his

185

father's. He's very skilled. Nonetheless, my mind took long to find peace as Enir would not permit me to remain by your side."

Thya smiled tightly. "I hope you did not cause trouble, Alkazar?" She raised her eyebrows and glared.

He changed the subject. "And is your mind at peace, my love?" he asked.

"'Tis," she replied.

Only Alkazar knew she was lying. Again, the light had gone from her eyes and they were now dull. He wondered if he would ever see her eyes shine again. Many times, through their stay with Enir, both Somal and Alkazar noticed, Thya get lost in thought. Staring at nothing of value and unable to snap out of it easily. Alkazar could only guess where Thya's mind went to on those occasions. When asked, she continued to deny anything was wrong. Whatever was conversed with Enir, she did not get her answers, or was not happy with the answers she got, he mused.

***

Soon it was time for them to depart and Enir gave Alkazar another silent lecture about respecting boundaries and to be there for Thya, as she would need his guidance. At least he would be required for something, he thought miserably.

The Torpas never had a ruler so why would they consider one now? Because Thya ordered it so, did not mean it would be. She was not their queen. Why would they heed her? Not one Torpas had disagreed with his own ideas and implementation, and certainly they treated him with respect, but they were Torpas not Tsinians.

It wasn't long before Alkazar recognized the welcome sight of the caves of Torpas. An iron gate raised halfway, waiting for them at the entrance into the mountain. To the left, Alkazar looked to see if he could see Calix up high in the guarding post beside the green forest. He smiled and quickened his pace, excited at the thought of seeing Omad and Galf again.

When they entered the Torpas caves, Thya noticed immediately that they were at least three times the size of Celdor Caverns. The entry was spacious and long, with many passages leading off to the left and the right. The shocked look on the Torpas' faces as they passed, made her smile stretch wider. Some fell to their knees and kissed the hem of her gown. Thya questioned if they had expected them to return from the quest. Yet it warmed her heart to see their reaction to Alkazar's presence, going down on one knee and kissing his hand, calling out his name with cheer. Yes, it was very unexpected, and she hoped he would receive the same welcome when they arrived back at Celdor Caverns. For now, she just wanted to bask in the love that was freely given.

Thya heard an echoed call coming towards her and recognized the voice. Her eyes lit up and her smile beamed when she saw him.

Omad went down on his knee and kissed Thya's hand before she pulled him up from the ground. "My queen, tis truly you? How well you sight. It has been much duration and I feared you would not return."

He embraced Somal and Alkazar and then stood

back, eyes wide and mouth open as he stared at each of them in turn.

Thya smiled and then embraced Omad. "Tis good to sight a familiar face, how do you fair?"

"Tis I that will inquire of you," he answered.

"As you can sight we are well, though we did not depart from Helkon as such."

"Will you take refreshment and inform me on all that occurred?"

"Nay, Omad. Alkazar will inform you on what transpired. I desire to pay homage to the Changlins. Will you escort me to where they dwell?"

"With certainty, tis fitting, my queen."

Again, Alkazar watched her eyes glaze over as she became still. He was convinced her sudden change had something to do with the Changlins. It was as though she did not want to visit the sacred stones. Her sigh and hunched shoulders confirmed his conclusion; Thya was forcing herself to visit them. But why?

Word soon spread of their arrival, and Alkazar was quickly reunited with Galf. Celebrations began. with music, singing, and dancing. Although he smiled and laughed with everyone, he couldn't truly relax as Thya had put her mask on again. She was doing a great job of pretending she was fine and having fun.

He moved closer to her and spoke quietly so only she would hear.

"My love, what troubles you? Why are you not rejoicing with everyone?"

"When I have attended to Kovon, and Tsinia is how it formerly was, then I will feel the want to celebrate."

"When do you intend to depart for Celdor

Caverns?" he asked.

"I am not certain on the duration. Pay no heed to me, for I am weary. I will rest. Will you join me?"

There are so many ways that her question could be construed. He would have preferred it to mean they would become one. That for a while her body would be his and, oh, the things he wanted to do with her. But sadly, this would not be the case. Too much was at stake and becoming one would be the last thing on her mind.

Alkazar accompanied Thya to her temporary bed chamber. He took her hand as she climbed onto the flat rock laden with pelts and soft blankets, then lay beside her. He held her hand and kissed her knuckles as he waited for her to speak. But patience was not one of his virtues.

"I am at your command, my queen. You appear pale and seem withdrawn. How can I ease your suffering?"

"I desire for you to address the Torpas. Inform them that they are welcome to unite with us and dwell in Tsinia."

"So, you intend to keep with your plan. Thya, the Torpas have existed unaided for much duration. Why would they consider your suggestion? They do not abide a dictator or heed to a code."

Thya sat up. "A dictator? I would never!"

"Possibly dictator is too strong a term. Alas, that would be what the Torpas thought. To suddenly be forced to live with rules for the first time in their existence."

"Alkazar, the Torpas once resided in Tsinia, did they not? They are Tsinian. It was their desire not to comply with the Tsinian code that pressed them to depart. I desire for them to be aware that an alternative is now given. I bestow to them the option. They will not be forced."

He let out the breath he didn't realize he was holding in and kissed her knuckle again. "I recall how I felt when I was informed that the Torpas did not conform to regulations. I believe I was liberated. It would be unwise for them to relinquish that independence."

Thya sighed. "You may be just. Though as I previously stated, tis their option. I cannot permit half of Tsinia to abide by the code and the other not. And I cannot disregard the code. What I ought to be capable of is to create alteration. I will converse with Pertius when we arrive at Celdor Cavern. At present, my head pains me too much for this to be of concern. I assign you to converse to the Torpas on my behalf. I hope they concur. Tis prudent for them to consider. Can you envision how magnificent Tsinia would become if the two lands unite? If they decide otherwise, I cannot protect them and look after their welfare."

"I will relay your suggestion, though I doubt they will be in accord. I am aware you intend to keep me active while you attend to Kovon. Why is that? Tis unsafe for you to venture to Senx unaided. Kovon awaits and I can only envision what his intentions are. Permit me to accompany you. I can employ my gift of Dispelling. He will not be aware of my presence and I bestow my oath that I will only interfere if I deem it necessary."

Thya sighed heavily. "I selected for you to converse

to the Torpas on my behalf because you have existed in both lands and can recognize the distinctions. They hold trust in you and will be attentive with open hearts and minds. Secondly, I will proceed to Senx unaccompanied and unaided and we will not debate this. And thirdly, Kovon will be aware and alert the instant I step on Senx. He would certainly discern if you were with me, whether you employed your gift or not."

"Your chances would be enhanced if you had assistance. How will you handle Kovon? What are you expecting? I desire to be informed, not as a concerned citizen but as your friend and future husband."

"There will not be debate. Respect my request. I will return. Did I not on the previous occasion?"

"With certainty, only Kovon possesses the power of the Dark Force."

Thya smiled. "You overlooked the mass of Rants he has protecting Senx and Tsinia."

"Precisely! How do you expect to fight them all? Even with your gifts you cannot stand unaided."

"Oh, dear Alkazar, how little trust you have in me. I do not stand unaided."

He tilted his head and waited for an explanation that did not come

"Do not dispute me. My head pains and I desire for calmness."

"My pardon, Thya. Rest and I will alleviate your pain."

She shut her eyes. "Inform the others that we will depart for Celdor Caverns at first light. Be certain you converse with Galf prior to our departure."

"Be assured it will be completed."

She laid her head on his lap and closed her eyes again. He massaged her temples and she sighed, within minutes, she fell peacefully into sleep.

***

Alkazar led the party on their journey to Celdor Cavern. This time without perils or obstacles to hinder them and they only needed to stop once for a short time to rest.

Thya was silent through most of the journey, only speaking when someone spoke to her. Alkazar watched her as she gazed at the beauty of the land, her eyes opening wider when she saw birds and ground creatures of Enumac.

Alkazar took her hand and caressed the skin with the side of his thumb. "When the conflict has ended, I desire to travel the Outlands with you," he said, and was rewarded with a smile that went straight to his aching heart.

Darkness had fallen by the time they arrived, and Thya instructed that no one was to be woken. Alkazar knew she needed headspace and time to compose herself before meeting her subjects as their queen for the first time.

He was woken by her attendant: Thya requested his presence. Alkazar washed, dressed and, after drinking a goblet of mouth-watering Tamin juice, he arrived. Chairs chiselled out of the mountain rock lined the sides of the cavern. It was used as an attendance room and was sparse, which made the place feel cold. Omad and Somal were already in attendance when he arrived. He bent down on one knee and waited for Thya to speak.

"Assemble my kinsmen for I desire to address them. I am certain they are impatient for responses. However, there are many occurrences and discoveries, which should remain between ourselves. You will inform them on what they are required to understand, naught further."

"It will be done, my queen." he answered, bowed once more, and left.

***

Omad stood beside Thya, Alkazar, and Somal, up on a raised platform and looked down at the anxious face of the citizens of Tsinia. Holding his hands aloft, he called out, "Be still, my friends." Once the chatter turned to whispers, Thya stepped forward.

"My kinsmen, we are triumphant, and the quest was met. However, the conflict is far from conclusion. As you sight, we are fortunate to welcome the return of Alkazar, son of Kapil, Tutor of the Arts. Through our travels, we have discovered the facts relating to Siren's demise and, in result of this, Alkazar had been absolved of all charges set against him. Omad and Somal, son of Valcan, perceived all and concur with my judgement. I desire for it to be recognized that Alkazar has reclaimed his gift of Dispelling and, furthermore, retains the gift of Illusor."

The cavern exploded into rapturous applause and, while Thya beamed proudly, Alkazar couldn't hide his surprise and delight. He was certain his face had turned red from embarrassment. He never expected this response.

Thya waited until the noise died before she continued. "Sorrowfully, Icas from the generation of Wecst was lost to us. If it were not for his unselfish sacrifice, we would not be present. Icas surrendered his existence for our cause. His sacrifice enabled us to persist in our battle. Icas will be remembered honourably.

"My honoured confidents will reply to your queries. However, before I depart, I desire to add. I retain certainty that within several Tril moons you will once more dwell on Tsinian soil. I intend to encounter Kovon and conclude his warmongering. I will retake Tsinia and restore it, creating a greater realm for all. Ought there be requirement for your involvement, I desire that you be prepared. Alkazar, Tutor of the Arts, will supervise your training. My kinsmen, I sight a glorious future ahead for all. We will be victorious."

The cavern erupted in deafening cheers and her name was chorused repeatedly.

Alkazar stood by her side, feeling proud of her. He remembered when she first stepped on Tsinia. Meek but stubborn. Thinking it was all a dream and she would wake up at home, in her bed. Even when she discovered the truth and learnt of her birthright, she refused to acknowledge and aid her kinsmen. And now presently, she was offering her life to save her kinsmen. Her powers could not be matched and although he did not understand where her second will came from, he believed she had control of it. Something had happened in Helkon. Maybe one day she would open up to him, trust him with the truth. He worried that their planned union would not take place, as she remained secretive. He understood the need for this, however, their union would be false if she did not reveal her darkest secrets.

Thya gestured to step down and he held his hand out to take hers but the Tsinians needed more answers.

"Where is the Darkeye?" one asked.

"It is lost," she replied.

The gathering took an intake of breath.

"Do not be concerned, the Darkeye is not required."

"Then how do we defeat Kovon?"

"I will proceed to Senx. Kovon is awaiting my arrival. I will settle our differences permanently."

Thya nodded and then took Alkazar's arm so he could lead her away.

"I wish to visit the Changlins," she said. "Do you believe my kinsmen have faith in me?"

"They would be silly not to. And those that may doubt, do not have knowledge of your newly-found power and skills."

She smiled, and he lifted her hand and kissed it.

"I will not fail them."

"I do not doubt that, my love."

Before entering the small stone alcove, she turned and held both of his hands.

"I received a premonition. Everything will work in my favour. Naught can stand in my way and I desire for you to know that and have faith in me. I admit freely that Kovon unnerves me. Tis as though he can see into the midst of my soul. Possibly he knows me better than I know myself. Back in Senx, he warned me not to destroy the Darkeye. He said I would be in requirement of it in the future. And he was correct. I do not know if he possesses the sight or that the Senx have their own Oracles."

Alkazar watched her body shiver and, just by reading her action, he knew her thoughts had gone dark.

"My love," he said, and lifted her chin.

She looked him in the eyes and said, "It was the second will that put those inflictions on Kovon. When it was concluded, I returned to myself, and he could no longer speak, hear, or see."

Alkazar gasped. It was the first time she had spoken about what had happened in Senx.

Stepping forward, she lifted her head and then continued. "I took away his senses and yet he survived and returned and took my land and my kinsmen's life hood. I should have removed his breath then. I will not make a similar error. Naught will alter until I make it so. The sooner I confront this evil warlord, the better. I will exist with my discovery and my future, but I am certain to retain peace once he is no more. He needs to disappear, so I can sleep without begin plagued by nightmares."

Alkazar caressed her cheek and gently kissed her lips. "My love, I have not doubt. You will be successful."

He left it until the following day before badgering Thya once again. It wasn't that he did not have faith in her being victorious. He just wanted her prepared for any outcome that might arise.

"Tis prudent to encounter Kovon as our queen?" he asked.

She shook her head. "Nay, tis not required. He is

aware, as are all. The coronation is just a formality."

"I am aware you will succeed and Tsinia will be restored, however following that? Have you opinions to the future, to the alterations you will create? Do you intend to revisit England?"

She sighed deeply. And then her eyes glazed over, her face screwed up, and her eyes closed. He cursed himself for giving her pain, reminding her of her home, back in England. She had enough to deal with without him adding dark thoughts to her mind.

"Nay, Alkazar, my mind is reeling. I have not considered the future. I desire to return to normality prior to this. However, I will return to England once more and require you to accompany me. I recall your excitement for my land. Does this still stand? There is much I desire for you to sight and discover. Will you come with me?"

"If this is what you truly desire?" he answered softly.

"How is that meant?"

"You have become remote of late. I sense you slipping from me. Am I losing you, Thya?"

"Oh, Alkazar, tis not true." She embraced him tightly and he squeezed her with just as much strength. Neither willing to let go.

She sighed. "All is such confusion and I am having difficulty putting it into perspective, though one thing is wholly apparent." She broke the embrace and looked into his face. "I love you and I can only face my future because you are in it. I confronted many upsetting things in Helkon, which I will not converse of, and you are the solitary reason I remain rational. Do not ever doubt my love, for I feel tis the only thing that maintains me.”

“Absolve me, Thya.” He bent down on one knee. “I did not comprehend. You have been locked away. I desire to aid you in your confusion. I will not rest as judge.”

Thya sighed and pulled him up from the floor. “I am not able. I recognize that I may never be. We each suffered anguish, and we each will deal with it in our own manner. Yet I pledge that, if need be, I will call upon you without delay.”

“’Tis fitting. I am present whenever you require me. And my love, I too cannot imagine my future without you by my side. If it were not for you, I would not have returned to Tsinia.”

She smiled, and it lit up her eyes. The sparkle he had wished for had returned.

Taking both his hands into hers, she gently squeezed them. “Each had a purpose on the quest and, if it was not for you, I would not be present.”

“I did not perform much,” he argued.

“I disagree. ’Tis the little things that matter most.” She smiled.

“At what duration do you desire for the coronation?”

She shrugged. “To be candid, I have not deliberated this. I desire to return to my land, and who can discern what duration will pass until Tsinia is restored.”

“How I yearn to sight England. Though I would not permit you to journey unaccompanied. In fact, I desire that you never depart from my side.”

“What you desire and what you acquire are different. Though you will accompany me to England, I do not require your service or company to Senx. I will proceed unaided and encounter Kovon alone. My kinsmen have suffered enough, and I will not involve them in this battle. I received the responsibility as ruler and I alone will restore Tsinia."

She was so stubborn, but that just made her more endearing to him.

He put his hands on his hips and raised his eyebrows. "We discussed this previously and I have not altered my view upon this. You will not proceed to Senx unaided, at the least bear an army with you."

Thya scowled. "An army? How do I employ an army without a citizen of Senx being unhurt? You have made your view very clear. Now you perceive mine." She stepped towards him and pointed her finger to his chest.

"I am your queen and you will accept my decision."

"Tis your command." He bowed and then left.

He could not argue with that. She was his queen and he had to obey her command. *Blast, I never wanted the night to end like this.* He wanted to lay with her in his arms and watch her sleep. Listen to her quiet snoring. But he understood she needed guidance from the Changlins. She had a prophesy to fulfil, yet again.

He laid awake for a long time before his eyes closed.

The next morning, Omad and Somal nagged Thya with their own complaints and, although Alkazar felt sorry for her, he decided not to say any more about it. She had made up her mind and, being Thya, there was no way she was going to back down.

"Do we remain until your return?" Omad asked. "When do you require for us to return to Tsinia?"

"You will recognize when the duration is correct.

You will understand the sign. Alkazar, I consign you to deploy a defence force; Omad, you will govern in my absence. Somal will be at your summons." They bowed their heads and then Thya called to Alkazar and took him aside.

"My love, do not fear for me for I am capable of defending myself."

"I am aware of this, though I will never understand where this newly-found confidence originates from. We will encounter one another again and I believe you will be victorious. Our souls are entwined."

"Kiss me. For I desire to taste your scent upon my lips as I proceed."

Who was Alkazar to deny the queen's order?

They embraced long and deeply. Whilst he held her in his arms he whispered, "I love you, Thya. Assure me you will not take any unnecessary risks."

"You retain my pledge. And I desire from you your word that you will watch over my kinsmen. Direct them well. I hold trust in you."

"I will act on my pledge, my queen."

Again, they held each other until Thya pulled away. She turned from him and began her solitary trek to Senx, never once turning back.

THYA'S VERDICT

Thya wasn't surprised to see Kovon's fortress looking the same as she remembered it. His abode, which his late father Darthorn had referred to as his castle, was built in the shape of a large gold dome and a long thoroughfare leading to a drawbridge was the only entrance and exit. The fortress stood at the top of the mountain of Senx, looking over what used to be the beautiful forest of Tsinia.

There were no armed guards by the open drawbridge. In fact, there were no guards, no servants, no citizens of Senx at all. The place was empty. Thya sensed a presence and yet didn't feel any threat; no hairs standing on end, no goose bumps. She had no fear. He was waiting for her and she knew exactly where to find him. She had been both a guest and a prisoner at the Senx fortress, so knew her way around.

Walls that were once richly decorated in gold were now covered in tarnished silver. They no longer shone and she wondered how long the fortress had been empty and neglected. Looking now at the cobwebs covering the dark and grey metal décor, Thya thought back to how rich and beautiful it looked when Darthorn was warlord. His father's rich and over-the-top design was preferable to Kovon's taste. Thya sighed. She looked straight ahead and walked faster, eager to finish this. Vengeance pulled her along.

Thya walked into the throne room and gasped. Dull metal sheeting and poles covered the wall of the great chamber. The rest of the décor was black or dark grey, giving the place a morbid yet powerful feel. A large window covered almost one side of the circular room.

She wasn't certain how she would feel about seeing Kovon, having put the inflictions she had on him. However, he was no longer blind, deaf, or unable to speak. Just one look at his sickening smile was enough to strengthen the loathing and hate.

"Thya, I have been waiting for you. You sight admirably."

"As do you, Kovon, and you will address me as Queen Thya, as is my right."

"And you will address me as Lord Kovon, as is my right." They had played this game before and yet there was more at stake this time. Thya glared at him.

"Queen Thya, how that title suits you. Even now you trigger my desires. The sight of you standing there in all your glory excites me. I always sought for you."

"I am aware of your desires, Lord Kovon. However, I have never been fond of domination games."

"One cannot pay a high price for any sensation. Do you concur?"

"Depends what sensation it is. I am informed that

your partners feel naught. Is that not the way you desire it?"

He ran his tongue over his top lip. "You ought to experience what my desires are."

"You will never pleasure me."

"I understand the thought of losing control frightens you."

Thya raised her eyebrows. "And the thought of losing control excites you."

Again, his tongue came out. He licked his bottom lip this time. "The line between pleasure and pain can be subtle."

Thya shook her head and sighed.

Kovon adjusted his position on the throne, sitting up straight. He glared at her. "King Theon is a gifted sorcerer, is he not? It was he that restored me. Did you locate what you were seeking?"

"I encountered Theon on more than one occasion."

"He assured me that you would not reach Helkon, although I understood better. You have not replied to my inquiry. Did you locate the Darkeye's twin?"

"Why? Are you nervous?" She smiled. "Do not fret, I did not locate the Darkeye's twin because it does not exist."

His eyes widened.

"It matters not. I do not require its power to defeat you. You are not alone with your newly-found power. I too gained a superior capability." Thya shook her head. "Nay, not the dark force." She pulled her shoulders back and stood straighter. "With your swell of might you are no contest. You disgust me. I cannot decide whether the affliction I put upon you repulses me more than your present face."

Kovon stood up from the throne. "The subsequent face you will sight, Queen Thya, will be the face of fatality itself." He laughed mockingly as he cast an incantation at her.

At that exact moment, she heard Alkazar scream in her mind. It was faint, she assumed because of the distance between them. The momentary lapse in concentration allowed the hex Kovon directed at her heart to throw her across the chamber. She slammed into the iron railings decorating the walls and crumbled to the floor. Kovon laughed and advanced towards her.

Her body was hot all over, as though her skin was being beaten with a whip of flames. Alkazar's screams continued she realized the burning pain was what *he* was experiencing. Tightness built in her chest, causing her to gasp. Her heart was slowing, no matter how hard she concentrated on regulating the beat. She blocked out the crushing pain and Alkazar's hurt, concentrating solely on the sound of her heartbeat. With every pulse, she finally realized she was dying.

Gritting her teeth and breathing deeply, she was determined to fight Kovon's hex and regain control. *I will not fail my kinsmen. I will not surrender hope.* For a fleeting moment, she considered eating the seed of hope. Was it the correct moment to consume the seed? The thought quickly passed. She did not require the seed of hope — she *was* hope. Hope for her kinsmen, hope for her son. Hope for every species that existed in Enumac. She would not fail. Then another thought occurred. How could she die if she was immortal?

I am immortal. I am … immortal. With every silently

repeated mantra, she felt her heart regulating. With every strengthening beat, she felt hope, power, love, and vengeance grow inside her.

Whether it was her own stubborn will, or that of the Gestle, it broke the hex. There was no way she was going to fail. At least, not before the battle. She owed her kinsmen that. Once she was certain she was in control and the danger had passed, she relaxed, closed her eyes, and laid still as the shadow of Kovon neared.

He knelt beside her. Holding her limp hand, he bought it to his cheek and caressed it, breathing in her scent.

"I am regretful for this outcome, my love. I believed there a future for us. It did not have to conclude this way. With my power and your appearance, we would have created a magical union. All would have been envious of our superior offspring and naught would have stood in our path."

He tossed her hand aside. "You contest me not. I was eager for a combat, not for your demise to conclude so swiftly. My father retained the correct notion. A new race - half Senx half Tsinian - and I will conclude his scheme. Once your kinsmen are enslaved, I will select a suitable candidate to bear my kin. What a warlord we would have created."

Kovon caressed the silk covering her legs. "What presented you with the notion that you could compete with me? Be satisfied that I concluded your existence swiftly. I could have prolonged your demise with agony and torture. My desire was to create suffering, yet I tire from the games and my schedule is precious. There are many punishments that need to be dealt."

Thya fought back the bile in her throat as he continued to touch her. Though his statement bought with it a picture of Alex playing happily with Alkazar, she could still sense Alkazar's pain. None were yet aiding him. Where was Somal?

She couldn't afford to waste any more time. She opened her eyes and sat up. Kovon fell back with surprise. He had barely time to stand before her will was upon him.

Thya had silently used her gift and froze Kovon where he stood. Although he had control of his thoughts, she could remove them just as easily.

"Are you excited at present, Kovon?" she mocked. "Prior to your demise, I desire for you to learn about who defeated the great Lord Kovon. Permit me to inform you on whom, or perhaps that ought it be, *what* I truly am."

She told him about the identity and power she owned in graphic detail before describing her final encounter with King Theon.

"My, Kovon, you seem to have misplaced your colouring. Not so exciting now, is it?" she taunted. "The disadvantage of my extraordinary power is that I did not get to recall or enjoy any of it. It seized full reign of me. Nevertheless, I desire to recall this conquest for eternity. Oh, and another small detail you are unaware of: I am immortal. You cannot destroy me." The last word came out as a growl. The Gestle's spirit had awoken.

Thya sensed Kovon's fear and consumed every drop of his terror. Only when she heard Alkazar cry out her name did she decide to end the confrontation.

There was no desire to allow him life a second time and no second thoughts about what she was about to do. A familiar burning and gathering of intense rage flowed through her body, only this time she allowed the Gestle spirit to take over but remained alert and focused.

Her vision sharpened as Kovon's appearance became a black silhouette with a bright red aura. This was the first time she had seen through the eyes of a Gestle. She laughed at the thought of her adversary looking like a bullseye target. She wondered if that's how all her victims looked before she destroyed them. A white beam emitted from the centre of Thya's eyes and a powerful blast hit Kovon. Her only thought was to destroy him.

The force hurled Kovon through the chamber window. Thya glided to where the window had stood and looked down. His body bounced from one jagged rock to another before his corpse, broken and mangled, landed at the boundary floor of Tsinia.

She turned and walked out of the hall without another thought for him. Not until she had rid every enemy from the soil of Tsinia would it be over. As tired as she was, she was ready to participate in the on-going battle, only first she needed to find Alkazar.

***

Alkazar lay under bushes, hidden from the enemies and unfortunately, his comrades. Although weak from injury to his ribs, he managed a smile as she rested his head on her lap.

"You held your duration," he joked.

"Silence yourself whilst I locate a healer to tend to you. Remain and I will dispatch aid presently."

"Would you abandon a fading Bora without a concluding kiss?"

Thya laughed. "You are distant from demise, Alkazar. Lie motionless until my return. As for the kiss, I can grant that."

She bent down and kissed him long and hard. And then broke away with a frown. "How can you be so jovial when fighting and peril surrounds us?"

"The moment I sensed your presence and sighted your radiant aura, I understood that all would be well. You return to me unharmed and Kovon is no more. Why not be jovial?"

"Then continue, except lie motionless, or you will cause yourself additional harm."

She left Alkazar still grinning and searched for Somal or Valcan.

The sound of spells whizzing in the air, steel clashing on steel, and yells from both sides ceased when they witnessed Thya's power.

Thya's eyes emitted a strong white light, anyone daring to look into her them felt like they were looking into a fire. Those that were now suddenly blinded had made that mistake. Screams and cries came from her victims as she moved in between the Tsinians, Senx, Torpas, and Rants. Thya only looked at those her demon self, chose to be guilty. The rest were unharmed.

Once the soldiers of Senx were surrounded, the Tsinians rounded them up. Thya struggled with her internal spirit. She closed her eyes tightly as she mentally willed the spirit to calm and to surrender, giving back full control. The Gestle was ready to destroy her enemies. The Rants recognized what she was the moment they saw her and so they fled. Not one Rant was stupid enough to take on a Gestle.

***

The beautiful rich green land of Tsinia was no more. All that remained was a burnt-out shell. The grounded buildings had been demolished so long ago, that little of the rubble remained. Blackened shadows were all that remained of Tsinia forest. Trees had been cut down and the tree houses, their homes, were no longer. Any possession they could salvage had been burnt. Only ash remaining. Even now, the smell of burnt wood lingered. As Thya looked at the carnage around her, tears fell.

The refreshing magical streams were almost empty of their unique water. Nothing would ever be the same again, Thya was sure about that.

Once the Tsinians explored and wept for their loss, they came together in discussion and it was the council that informed Thya that, even though their homes were no more, they were adamant they were going to spend the night on their own land. Thya argued, assuming that the Tsinians wouldn't find peace on the ground, without shelter. But her kinsmen wouldn't back down and refused the warmth and shelter of the caves.

There was so much to do and all were eager to begin. However, Thya wanted to start her reign off right. She wanted Tsinia to be better than before and that required a lot of planning.

NEW BEGINNINGS

The Tsinians did not take to change easily but, with careful explanation of her plans and with the backing of loyal friends, they accepted her ideas. She was their queen. Though she had yet to be crowned, she had saved them more than once and they felt they owed her everything, especially their allegiance.

Thya watched the door being fitted to the Plecky, amazed at how quickly Tsinia was being rebuilt. The speed at which the Tsinians and Torpas worked showed Thya how determined they were to restore their land to its former glory. Thya instructed that the Upess and the Plecky were to be built just as before. Both places were special to her. The Upess was where she was first introduced to her kinsmen and shown their unique powers; and the Plecky was where the sacred stones were housed. Yes, stones. That was all they were, but she needed to keep up the pretence as her kinsmen needed normalcy and it would be wrong of her to take away their hope and faith.

Thya sighed. Things would never be as they once were. The beautiful forest of Tsinia was no more. Grenko could regrow the forest but only as small tress. It would take years for the forest to be as it once was. For now, small wooden houses had been built from the wood of the ancient trees that had not been turned into ash. The Tsinians had lived within the branches for centuries, before being forced to hide in caves, and now they were forced to reside on the ground. Thya was proud of her kinsmen. There were no tears, no moans, and the smiles gradually returned. They chatted and joked as they spent many Tril moons rebuilding Tsinia. The lakes were poisoned black, but she knew that with the gifts of the Tsinians and the magic of the land, love would return to it and the lakes would run turquoise again. That thought made her mouth move into a genuine smile.

She greeted everyone as they worked and then her mind turned to England and Alex. She wondered if he had grown while she'd been away. Brushing away a fallen tear, she exhaled a shaky breath as she envisioned running up to her boy and him crying and hugging his grandmother's legs as he wouldn't recognize her anymore. So much time had passed and, although she was eager to return home to Alex, she wouldn't leave until she was certain her kinsmen were safe and that Tsinia was once again stable. Thya hoped that would be true sooner than later.

***

Thya recalled the first time she had been seated in the

stands of the Upess, and her first experience of the Lupa tournament. It had been a long time since the stands were filled with joyful voices. Nevertheless, there she was, the centre of attention again, thirty Tril moons after taking back Tsinia. Her citizens were dressed in their finery and there was an array of refreshments on wooden tables, waiting to be eaten. Thya was just as anxious as the first time she was there.

Dressed in a gold silk gown that draped loosely off her shoulders, she walked hand in hand with Alkazar towards Omad.

She had once renounced her title, leaving most of Tsinia believing this day would never come. With no regrets and no second thoughts, she allowed the golden leaf crown to be placed on her head. Although she had accepted the title, it was a relief for many to make the position official.

Thya soaked in the cheers and cries as they rejoiced but her smile faltered when 'Praise the Changlins' was called out. For the sake of appearances, she beamed a smile and waved. She needed to keep the truth from everyone. She had no intention of revealing to any Tsinian, including Alkazar, that the Changlins were mere stone chambers and that it was her spirit who commanded them. Would anyone even understand? Who would they turn to in need? And what would they believe in instead? No! It was better if they continued in their belief of these sacred stones.

As with all Ganties, once she allowed people to refer to her royal title, that was the acceptance. The placing of the crown was a formality and wasn't normally done in front of spectators. Only this was different, so she had been told. Tsinia had never had a Ganty like her. They never had a ruler that had fought the Dark Force and on more than one occasion. What she had done for them, they could never repay. She was their saviour, and they gave thanks to the Changlins for returning her and bestowing this great power…

If only they knew.

"Tsinians, your queen declares that I happily and wholeheartedly accept the responsibility as ruler of Tsinia, guardian of the Changlins and Warden of Senx. I vow that I will create an improved and superior Tsinia and that I bestow protection to all who require it. To our neighbours above. The Senx, will exist without a warlord and will govern themselves. As warden, I promise to watch and protect the citizens of Senx. The Torpas have agreed to remain in Tsinia for the present. While they reside within our borders, I will act as warden and watch and protect them. This is my oath."

The only thing ruining the moment was that she knew how false and fake the spectacle was. She felt physically sick from the lie she was keeping from them. She would never truly feel she was their queen until she could be open and honest. Only she had to live with the guilt. No one could ever learn she was immortal.

Though the crowning was short, the celebrations lasted throughout the night. Just like past festivals she had been involved in, she observed that the Tsinians knew how to enjoy themselves. Thya kept the smile on her face, though her heart was aching. She swayed to the beat of the music although, in truth, she would had preferred to sit still. When dragged up to dance, she held the hand of the person to her left and right and danced around with them, but there was no joy. Thya stayed as long as her head would allow it. The pounding drums, the loud laughter was ringing through her head, causing an almost blinding headache. When she stood to leave, Alkazar was by her side, leaving the villagers to continue their celebrations.

Alkazar escorted Thya to the newly-built Recas, which was more elaborate than the last. This castle was the size of a four-bedroom house but with turrets and a gated drawbridge. It was a little over-the-top, but she was a queen and wanted a castle, even if it was tiny.

Alkazar stood by the door, waiting for her to give him the okay to go in. They had not spent a night together since returning to Tsinia, which was Alkazar's doing. He believed it wasn't right for him to spend a night in her chamber until they were married. It had never mattered to him before, so why now? He paced outside while he waited for her to say something. She knew she needed to, but it was also the last thing she wanted.

"I am weary, Alkazar. I desire for slumber. Call upon me early light for we ought to converse."

Alkazar bowed his head.

"'Tis your command, my queen."

She heard sadness in his tone but chose to ignore it. Before she had turned to enter, Alkazar had already walked away.

***

Her eyes fluttered open to find Alkazar sitting on the edge of the bed watching her.

"Tis light already?" Thya whispered.

He reached down and caressed her cheek. "You did not rest soundly. I will summon for Valcan."

"Nay, do not burden Valcan unnecessary. He is mature, and I desire for him to reduce his duties. I will invite Somal to become my advisor. He will perform most of Valcan's responsibilities."

"Tis fitting," he agreed. "I am not aware of another Tsinian who deserves the title."

"Do you suppose he will accept?"

"With certainty, tis a great honour."

Alkazar stood up to leave but Thya held onto his arm. "Nay remain. Is there a code that forbids a companion to call upon his potential spouse?"

He smiled. "There is not."

"And is it permitted for the queen to slumber late on occasion?"

"With certainty," he mused, still not getting the drift.

She sighed and patted the empty side of the bed. "Then join me, Alkazar. We will not be disturbed."

It had been a while since they had made love and she didn't want it to end. When they were as one, she could forget all her worries. Only whilst lying in his arms did she feel safe.

After they dressed, they ate breakfast on the balcony.

"I was pondering," she said whilst picking at the sweet bread. "The coronation formalities are complete so there is naught evading us from wedlock. What do you suppose to three moons? That ought to present us enough duration for arrangement."

"I was eager to discuss our matrimony," he replied. "There is something you ought to be aware of concerning the ceremony."

Thya put down the sweet bread she'd been nibbling on and listened attentively.

"'Tis basic, dissimilar to what you are familiar with."

He seemed to have forgotten she was present when he and Siren were married. She didn't bother reminding him.

"On entering the Plecky we pledge our love, loyalty, and respect of each other to the Changlins."

She shivered at the mention of the Changlins and bit her lip nervously. A chill covered her skin and her good mood vanished.

Alkazar frowned. "What ails you, Thya? Whenever the Changlins are spoken of, you freeze."

"I am weary, and you did mention you would summon Somal for me."

"Very well, though I sense an alteration of conversation. I realize that you do not want to unburden your troubles onto me, however prior to becoming one, we are obliged to disclose all our secrets. For the union to be honourable, we are required to reveal all to one another, in the presence of the Changlins."

The notion of revealing her darkest secrets to Alkazar didn't bear thinking about.

"You retain secrets, Alkazar?" she said, attempting to lighten the mood.

"One, which I will maintain until our union."

"Summon Somal, Alkazar, for I require a healer."

Alkazar left without another word, which gave her time to consider what he had said.

Could she wed Alkazar, being fully aware that her

life was a lie, a sham, just as her coronation was? Could she live with herself? Nay, she loved him too much and she needed him. She needed his support and she could not have him, all of him, unless they became one. There was much to think about and only three Tril moons to decide.

A distant bell sounded, and a light rap on the door awoke her from daydreaming. Somal entered seemingly out of breath.

"You did not sprint the entire journey?" she joked to Somal. "'Tis not fatality." She smiled.

"Alkazar, bade me to attend to you without delay and so with haste I appear."

"And I am grateful."

"How can I aid, my queen?"

"As you can imagine my mind has been disturbed."

"Pardon me if I address in error. However, I believe it has been some duration since you rested well."

"Naught passes you, Somal."

"My father's potion will ease your suffering."

"Nay, on this occasion your gift will suffice."

He laid his palm over the top of her eyes and she fell into a dreamless sleep.

***

Thya allowed two Tril moons to pass before coming to a decision. She wanted the time and setting to be just right for her declaration and so arranged a picnic at hers and Alkazar's favourite spot, the only place where you were unseen, the crystal blue lake.

Once the city was again under Tsinian rule, the

enchanting streams had refilled themselves and the shrubbery surrounding the picturesque setting flourished. It was as if the environment had come back to life the moment the Tsinians retook their land. The poison Kovon had injected evaporated.

Unfortunately, their conversation didn't get off to a great start. She had been filled with nothing but thoughts of what and how she was going to say what she wanted to say, so that when it came to it, she blurted it out.

"I will not wed you, Alkazar."

Alkazar stepped back. It looked as though he wasn't breathing.

"I deliberated firm on this," she continued. "I will not enter a false union and that is what it will be. I will not reveal my secrets to you. Some things are best undisturbed."

"I understand, Thya and I am grateful for your openness. However, if we do not cement our union how are we to be together? How are we to create a family?"

Her stomach fluttered.

"We will wed," she said. "However, it will not be a Tsinian matrimony or even held in Tsinia. I desire more than anything to become your companion. Still, I will not exist with falsehood."

What was she saying? Her whole existence was false. "We will return to England and create our union there. I can obtain a license and credentials for you without inquiry and we can return to Tsinia ahead of an Earth week."

Alkazar's smile lit up his face. "You have considered

this then. I would prefer our union to occur in Tsinia. Nevertheless, if you do not desire this, then so be it. I yearn for you to be my life companion and if it is legitimate, whether Earth custom or Tsinian, then it is agreed by me. I am certain the Changlins will concur, though I am not certain that the council will form an understanding."

"I conversed with the Changlins," she quickly answered, "and they are content with our arrangements. Do not fret. I will manage the council. I am grateful, Alkazar, I believed you would be sympathetic. I too am eager to become your life companion, and to be aware in my heart, that the union will be just and genuine."

***

Thya felt it was the right time to reveal to the council and her citizens the biggest change in her plans for Tsinia. Although she was certain that it wouldn't receive a good response, she was adamant that these changes would be put into place.

The following morning the council convened in the newly-built Escos. The inside was similar to the original Escos. The dome allowed circled, high seating for the council members and the large yellow star on the floor, was placed as it always was, in the centre of the dome.

Omad held his arm out and escorted Thya to the throne within the stoned circle, but her seat was raised so none would forget she had the power in that room. This was how it had always been and how it would continue, Thya decided.

"Alkazar has returned from the caves of Torpas

with a response to a proposition I prepared previously," she announced after the council reseated.

The members shifted in their chairs. She had yet to speak to them about her proposal.

"You have yet to encounter a Torpas. They sight as you and possess similar gifts as ourselves. The solitary difference between our two species is that the Torpas exist without a code and endure with this system. I believe tis prudent for the Torpas to unite with us. We will develop into a stronger, greater Tsinia and the two will prosper." She looked into the face of each council member, before continuing. "I did not summon you for permit. I called for this congress to notify you of a decision I have arrived at."

She waited for the murmurs to quieten. "The Torpas exist happily devoid of a code and I cannot expect them to suddenly exist in a land govern by rules. And I have no intention of ending the Tsinian code. Therefore, I am resolute that the code will be modified."

The intake of breath and everyone talking at once was the kind of response she expected.

Tasark stood up. "My queen, the code is ancient and has never been modified. Why alter it presently? Cannot the Torpas exist in union with our convention, if tis truly your desire?"

"I am not aware that the code forbids alteration. I am not going to conclude our laws. I would never entertain such notion. Modification is inevitable for the creation of a stronger Tsinia. The Torpas will need to feel comfortable, and I propose these alterations will be beneficial to Tsinia. I sense your un-assurance and I am willing to respond to all your queries. It will be beneficial for our two nations to unite. As I previously stated, Alkazar has returned from the caves of Torpas and they are considering my proposal. Provided the alterations are acceptable to them. Understand that the undertaking the Torpas will have is colossal. It will be a challenge for them to exist amid any laws. I anticipate every kind heartedness and concern will be displayed to the Torpas on their arrival and I expect you both to exist in harmony.

"Pertius retains the modernized code, which he will now interpret. I will remain and will respond to your uncertainties."

After Pertius had finished reading the new code he rolled up the scroll, sat down on his chair and waited. There was a moment's stunned silence before the disagreements began.

Thya was adamant that not one of her citizens would find themselves in the same situation as Alkazar once did and scrapped the code for removal of existence. And no one would be forced into a union that they did not want, especially as she now had the power to know whether a union was suitable or not.

With every new moon she was discovering new awakenings to her abilities, though she had yet to accept them, she was finding some of them useful.

***

Light was ending and Alkazar located Thya in her chamber, laid out on a divan in a dark room.

"My Queen, are you unwell?" he called

She sat up. "I shut my eyes, save for a moment. Am

I required?"

"Nay. Continue to rest, all is well. Why the shade though?"

"'Tis how I favour it. It conveys ease."

Alkazar sat beside her and took one of her hands into his. "What ails you my love, for you slumbered much duration?"

"You are in error. I barely closed my eyes."

"Thya, dark will shortly fall."

Thya's brows furrowed, and as Alkazar opened the shutters to prove how late it was, she squeezed her eyes shut and pressed a hand to her head. Even the last of the Tsinan light was too much for her.

"I am the only Bora on Enumac you ought not worry about, Alkazar. I will summon Somal presently."

He shook his head. "'Tis not required. For I have already done so."

A bell rang out, announcing Somal's arrival. He entered the room with a low bow. "My queen, you are in requirement for your healer?"

"Alkazar seems to consider so," she answered and attempted a smile. "'Tis naught I am certain, save fatigue."

"And what is the cause of this fatigue, I wonder?" Somal quizzed.

"Exactly," Alkazar jumped in, "there is little that requires your hand, and your plans for Tsinia are almost complete."

Thya sighed deeply. "Perhaps that is the explanation. The effort and stress has finally caught up with me. As I state, tis naught."

"Permit me to be the evaluator," Somal answered.

He rested his hands on Thya's brow and concentrated hard. "Tis bizarre," he said after a moment.

"What is?" she asked, noticing how Alkazar's eyes widened and his face lost its colour.

"I cannot heal your exhaustion, Thya, as I cannot sense the source."

"I informed you tis naught. More likely emotional."

"I concur, my queen. Save, I would sense that too. Do not be concerned. I am certain my father's potion will remedy your ills. Rest, and I will obtain it. Alkazar, a moment if you will."

Alkazar made sure she was comfortable and lightly kissed her forehead as Thya closed my eyes. They spike outside, but the door was left ajar. And although their conversation was hushed, she was able to hear them.

"Speak freely, my friend," Alkazar urged.

"I believe tis prudent you depart for England almost immediately. Thya is in requirement of recuperation and I deem an adjustment in scenery will suffice. Pardon me if I converse insolently."

"Nonsense, Somal, there is naught you could utter that would offend or be in error and I will act on your suggestion. I depart this instant and commence the planning for the queen and my departure. I am grateful for your remark, my friend."

"Do not converse of Tsinia while absent. Tis prudent that Thya is permitted complete forgetfulness for at least for some duration. And make no haste to return."

***

Somal returned with a draft of his father's potion. She struggled to open her eyes, but Somal insisted. "Partake in this potion, my Queen."

She took the bottle and drank the bitter liquid.

"It does not do well to dwell on the past," Somal told her and in return, received a smile.

"Somal, you sighted and perceived my darkest secrets and I can only imagine the torture you suffered in the hands of the Rants. I am indebted to you. Though what I can bestow onto you is my devotion and respect. I desire for your father to half his duties and for you to present yourself as the Tsinian healer. I am aware of your capabilities. I also desire for you to accept the position as my personal mentor. I am in requirement of someone whom I can trust and rely on and I cannot suppose of someone better to retain by my side and confide in. There are still modifications I desire to create and much responsibility. I trust I can rely upon you to aid me."

"I am honoured that you considered me, though I am not certain I am the correct Tsinian to fulfil your requirements. Nonetheless, if tis your desire then so be it. I graciously accept your elevation and I am optimistic that I will embrace all your expectations."

"I have not expectation, Somal."

He bent down on one knee and took her hand. "Summon for my service, my Queen, for I am at your disposal. Alkazar is currently planning your departure at my request; I expect that on your return we will converse. You can rely upon me for discretion."

It had been a long time since Thya had felt like crying, but after Somal left, that's just what she did.

Only, once she started, she couldn't stop, and all the hurt and confusion that had been eating her up inside flooded out.

Though she slept, it wasn't peaceful. Her thoughts were plagued with indecision and, on waking, she knew it couldn't be put off any longer. She had to tell Alkazar about his son, and in doing so she hoped to release some of the stress that was causing this unusual fatigue. Unusual in the sense that, for the first time, Valcan's wonder potion didn't help in any way. It wasn't a typical tiredness. She felt achy and drained, more so than she had the previous day.

After a hearty breakfast, she summoned for Alkazar.

"We depart for England next light. I have been meaning to inform you on something, only I wanted it to hold off until Tsinia was stable. Well, normality has been restored and I cannot delay longer. Nay, tis not what you suppose. It has to do with our return to England."

Alkazar took her hands. "Steady your breathing and commence gradually, when you are prepared."

She took a deep breath first. "The foremost reason for your accompanying me, is there is someone I desire for you to encounter. I have not declared of him as yet, as I was not certain whether I would remain or return to England." She stopped and took another deep breath. "I was with child on my departure from Tsinia, though I was unaware. He is named Alex and he is three Earth years, at least he was when I departed."

Alkazar fell to his knees. "I possess a son?" He wept. "Can it be possible, inform me of him I beg of you."

Thya smiled. "He is a fine boy. He's intelligent and boasts your eyes. I believed he was my final bond to you. I have considered this deeply and I desire for him to return with us and exist as a Tsinian. As is his birthright."

"Tis fitting, Thya. Though why the deliberation?"

"I am taking his childhood from him. Believe me, it was a taxing decision."

Alkazar paced the room excitedly.

"It will be some duration prior to his coming of age and I am not certain what the occurrence will be as this had not occurred previously. He will be taught the code and his gifts… Oh, Thya, imagine, a son of yours will be unique. I marvel at what gifts he will possess."

Thya had wondered about that. Now that she had learnt about the Gestle spirit and had witnessed her extraordinary power, it frightened her to imagine what genes she may have passed onto Alex. If he remained on Earth he would never learn of his ancestors or his birthright, only she had accepted the crown and pledged to remain in Tsinia and she could not do that without Alex. Yes, it was a difficult decision to make, and yet she was certain it was the right one.

"Alkazar, he is not acquainted with Tsinia, yet I converse of you often. He is save, a child and I doubt he would understand."

"Oh, what blissful tidings. We ought to assemble the council and inform them."

"Nay," she shouted and held onto his arm. "I prefer for this to remain between ourselves until his arrival. You cannot imagine the fear I held whilst on Earth. Not only was I fearful that a Senx would hunt for me,

I was afraid the council would learn of Alex and that he would be taken from me."

He gasped. "That would never have occurred."

"Even so, the fear was instilled. When Alex was born the risk became greater. The contemplation of having to return without him was choking me."

"Thya, my love, you have survived more than any Tsinian ever will in their whole existence. Tis your strength that will aid you in your acceptance of what you discovered in Helkon."

"Possibly, yet as Enir stated, only duration will tell."

"A son," Alkazar repeated, his mouth remaining open.

She stepped up to him, giggled and then closed his lips.

He laughed, and they embraced, before he swung her around yelling, "A son!"

It seemed a long time since she had looked forward to the future and it was looking brighter every day.

***

Thya and Alkazar's farewells were jovial compared to the last time she had left Tsinia, when she believed Alkazar was dead and had nothing but sad memories. On this occasion, he was by her side and, though her time in Enumac wasn't exactly pleasant, it was home. She was leaving a newly-built city full of promise, and a happy nation, which, for the first time, felt safe and carefree.

"How do you feel?" Alkazar asked.

"Happier than I thought I could ever feel. I am

looking forward to returning. And you, my love?"

"I confess I am nervous. I am heading for an encounter with my son for the first instance, and although I studied your world, I am unacquainted with what to expect. I am nervous with anticipation. I have not rested for many Tril moons. Tis a like to a dream and, from what you described and explained, it sounds magical, full of adventure and astonishment."

Thya laughed.

"Tis how I considered Tsinia when I first arrived. I would not describe Earth as such. There is much for you to sight, Alkazar, yet it would take an existence to do so. Nevertheless, I am returning to collect our son and cement our union. I desire not to linger. Tsinia is my home. I have naught to remain in England for, in addition there is still much to complete here."

The opaque opal shaped orb appeared. Thya grabbed hold of Alkazar's hand and squeezed tightly. He took a deep breath and stepped forward.

The End

Reviews are important to an author so please take a moment to leave a rating and review:

ACKNOWLEDGEMENTS

A huge thank you to my editor Michelle Dunbar. This lady has so much patience and has supported me through this long and somewhat difficult journey and she's been my rock.

Thank you to my publisher, Asteri Press, for taking a chance on my duology, believing in me, and the books.

ABOUT THE AUTHOR

Karina Kantas is the author of the popular MC thriller series, *Outlaw* and the loved romantic fantasy duology, *Illusional Reality.*

She also writes short stories and when her imagination is working overtime, she writes thought-provoking dark flash fiction.

There are many layers to Karina's writing style and voice, as you will see in her flash fiction collection, *Heads & Tales* and in *Undressed* she opens up more to her fans, giving them another glimpse into her warped mind.

When Karina isn't busy working on her next bestseller, she's helping authors with *Author Assist*, working full time as publicist, author manager, VA, and narrator. She's also the host of a popular radio show Author Assist on the Artist First Radio Network.

Karina writes in the genres of fantasy, MC romance, Young Adult. sci-fi, horror, thrillers and comedy.
Her inspirations are the author S.E.Hinton and the rock band, Iron Maiden.

Amazon Author Page: http://bit.ly/KarinaKantas

Sign up to Karina's mailing list and you will receive a free gift: http://bit.ly/KKAML